THE PANDEMIC LIFE OF A MIDWESTERNER

Proof that quality of life is all about perception and that you really can laugh at just about anything, even yourself, if you try hard enough.

Cory Eckert

Copyright © 2020 Cory Eckert

No part of this book may be reproduced, or stored in a retrieval system, or transmitted in any form or by any means, electronic, mechanical, photocopying, recording, or otherwise, without express written permission of the publisher.

ISBN-13: 9798673323304

Cover design by: Cory Eckert
Printed in the United States of America

INTRODUCTION

The Pandemic Life of a Midwesterner is a journal of sorts, kept by Cory Eckert while he and his family were living life at its strangest in rural America for the better part of 2020 during the CoronaVirus pandemic.

Inside, you'll find proof that quality of life is all about perception and that you really can laugh at just about anything, even yourself, if you try hard enough.

These short daily accounts came complete with images in their original form.

Be sure to join our Facebook group for the full experience!
https://www.facebook.com/groups/pandemicinthemidwest

On January 1st, 2020, AKA the good ole days when 2020 was just a normal boring year like any other, my family and I were enjoying a new acreage we had just moved into and we were, much like the rest of the world, blissfully unaware of what was to come in the months ahead.

Fast forward to Thursday March 19nd 2020 and we all witnessed the beginning of the turd tornado that would be 2020. Things were gonna get sloppy and we all had a front row seat.

March 19th the first stay at home order in the US was issued in California in an attempt to "flatten the curve" of the CoronaVirus.

That was day 79 of the year 2020. Twenty three days later, I started an online journal to keep track of our pandemic experience and to help pass the time.

What follows are my daily adventures as recorded on the day, uncut, unedited, and raw for your consumption.

Images available at - **https://www.facebook.com/groups/pandemicinthemidwest**

YEAR OF THE PLAGUE DAY 112:

Today's accomplishments...

I started the day by letting the same dagom cat out of a live trap for the second time in 24 hours. This was her fourth time in the trap this week and I'm beginning to question her mental health.

Used up a bunch of gas in the chainsaw taking down and chopping up three trees.

Removed a full truckload of scrap wood from the shed and tree grove. All the trees and scrap wood were stacked and burned into a small pile of ash.

Put the sprayer on the 4 wheeler and sprayed the yard for weeds.

Started peeling some crazy ass vines out of the trees. I'm not too sure what they are but they are tearing up the trees so down they come.

State of the Compound

The women folk are doing well. Teresa is keeping herself busy by painting pretty much everything and Hannah is staying occupied with homework and whatever the hell it is she does on her phone all day.

Remi the lab is doped up on anti seizure meds and she's basically a mindless zombie all day.

Liberty, the golden retriever, is a teething puppy with a Napoleon complex who needs constant attention.

The outdoor cats are fat and happy (except the one black cat who tried to cross the road and did not succeed). The fat momma cat is about to pop so we are watching her closely.

Most Recurring Thought for Today

My fat ass needs a few less snickers and a few more sit ups. I was ready for a nap by noon and that just won't do.

Message to Outsiders

Think what you like about where this whole virus started, I think it came from that bitch Carole Baskin.

Stay safe out there folks, it's a strange new world!

YEAR OF THE PLAGUE DAY 113:

Today's accomplishments...

Started out today by letting another cat out of a live trap not intended for cats. At least it was a different cat this time.

Made Teresa some gates for the porch to allow the dogs to enjoy it with us and keep them out of trouble. I'm sure Teresa can stain them later to match the rest of the porch.

State of the Compound

The women folk made a meal plan for the next few weeks and devised a shopping list from that meal plan.

Teresa saddled up the Malibu and braved the local shops to forage for all the items we needed.

Hannah, on the other hand, decided to shave part of her eyebrow out of boredom and we convinced her it was a gang sign and she needs to never do that again.

The cat we caught in the live trap today is called Ginger. We named her months ago, but today with her in the trap, we found out that Ginger is a dude.

Ginger is now called Garfield and will be losing his marbles later this summer.

Thanks to an anonymous tip, I found out the vines I wrestled with yesterday were in fact poison ivy. Maybe it's dumb luck or maybe I have poison ivy super powers but it didn't seem to affect me in any way.

Remi the lab is still doped up but Liberty is keeping her active by chewing on her face at every opportunity.

Liberty is loving the freedom of the porch and disappears for half an hour at a time which has been great for the overall morale within the home.

Momma cat disappeared for a few hours today but she finally showed up. Hannah seemed to be relieved and showed the first signs of happiness since finding out she has a gang sign on her face.

Most Recurring Thought for Today

If I didn't have kids to pick on, I would have been divorced so long ago. On the other hand, If I had smarter kids, I wouldn't have so much ammo to use against them.

Message to Outsiders

Be wary of climbing vines and never trust a ginger!

YEAR OF THE PLAGUE DAY 114:

Today's accomplishments...

With the great weather came great responsibility. A lot more trees needed to come down and a lot more brush needed burned.

A pile of poison ivy the size of a car was also removed and disposed of. This time gloves were worn before handling the ivy.

After catching another cat, this time with no bait in the cage, I decided our cats were too retarded to have traps set up in this area. All traps are packed back up in the shed.

The nice weather has inspired the grass to grow at an unreasonable rate. While the brush pile was burning, I bounced around on the mower for about 3 hours and got it all mowed. It seems I will be spending a good part of my summer on that mower.

A spot in the barn has been located for our new chickens who are set to arrive next month. I'll get to cleaning that spot up in future updates.

State of the Compound

Teresa put together our new hitch so we could go get the camper. I inspected her work and I believe she has a bright future in the business of nut handling.

Hannah didn't do much today. She may have spent some time on her phone talking with some guy named Ihack or Ballsack or something like that.

Hannah insists his name is Isaac but I refuse to be drawn into a game of "Toe May Toe" or "Toe Mah Toe" with a gang member.

Efforts will be made to keep her busy over the weekend and refocus her attention. I wonder if this Ballsack character had anything to do with her shaved eyebrow??

I managed to singe my beard and my eyebrows while tending the brush pile fire today. I spent the next 4 hours smelling burned hair and wondering what had made me go down wind of a large fire to add more brush.

The cats were doing well today. While Teresa was assembling our hitch, two of the cats got into the shop. I spent the next 15 minutes trying to herd them back out.

Just as they were at the door and ready to walk out, Teresa came around the corner and spooked the crap out of them. We did eventually get them herded back to safety.

Remi the lab got some doctoring today after Liberty put a few holes in her by playing rough with her sharky puppy teeth.

Liberty the golden retriever is still a little handful and her cuteness is literally the only thing keeping her alive at this point.

Most Recurring Thought for Today

Does burned hair always smell this bad or does grey hair smell worse than normal hair when burned?

Message to Outsiders

Always approach a fire from upwind.

YEAR OF THE PLAGUE DAY 115:

Today's accomplishments...

Today we kept accomplishments to a minimum in observation of "I'm too damn tired to move" day.

We did however get our bug-out home out of storage. If for any reason we run low on ammo and can not hold the compound during the apocalypse, we are prepared to live on the road.

By on the road, I mean in well maintained state campgrounds with full hookups. We're willing to rough it but let's be reasonable here.

State of the Compound

My sense of smell is starting to slowly return and I can smell things other than my own burning hair.

To my disappointment, I found I have a character flaw and I am not as "rustic" as I once believed. The truth is, I'm a fair weather farmer and all activities were canceled today due to rain. My exhaustion and shame kept me occupied for the remainder of the day.

Teresa and Hannah were watching Dr. Pol on Hulu and continued to say "Awe" every 15 seconds. The 85 year old Dr. Pol was wrestling cows and other animals like he's 20 years old.

I feel like this show may be working against me in terms of what Teresa believes a guy's energy level should be.

The dogs appeared to share my appetite for naps today and took advantage of the quiet time. Liberty still had her moments but they were short lived today.

Most Recurring Thought for Today

Is it bedtime yet?

Message to Outsiders

Know your limits and filter what your loved ones watch on TV.

YEAR OF THE PLAGUE DAY 116:

Today's accomplishments...

Teresa worked on sanding and painting her cabinet doors a little today, but for the most part, accomplishments were limited to not accomplishing much.

We did enjoy the day so I guess that's an accomplishment in itself.

State of the Compound

With all of our recent activity, the local deer and turkey decided to come look at the new people in the neighborhood. They walked right through the yard like they owned the place.

We are starting to see them more often which I can only attribute to them enjoying the comedy act that is my life. Come to think of it, they must be telling their friends because we keep seeing more of them as of late.

Teresa has taken up her Tiger Queen training with the kittens and has been hinting at the tiny tiger's appetite for human flesh. I'm not sure how to take that but I'll be keeping an eye on the situation moving forward.

Hannah had a bit more get-up-and-go today so we talked her into taking our first family fishing trip to the lake. She was pleasant to be around and showed little sign of that teenage charm her age group is so famous for.

Remi had to stay home because she can't wear a collar at the moment but Liberty got to experience a lake for the first time and she seemed to enjoy the experience.

It was a bit windy and cold but I think we spent the Sunday as well as a Sunday can be spent.

Most Recurring Thought for Today

I should shoot that and eat it!

Message to Outsiders

We're not social distancing, we just don't like you.

YEAR OF THE PLAGUE DAY 117:

Today my friends, was a full day.

At precisely 6:15 AM Liberty woke me up to feed her. Never mind that I'm the human and she's the dog, Liberty wants what Liberty wants.

Since I was already up and in possession of the kind of energy only the desire to kill a dog can drive, I set my sights on digging a hole for our new mailbox instead.

I gathered my coffee and my tools and set off on the long walk to the end of the drive to teach some dirt a thing or two about a thing or two.

As luck would have it, that dirt was mixed pretty heavily with asphalt and the lessons being learned were not those I had in mind.

I did discover a new swear word today... "sonofamothergoddamnrockhardassfuckerbitch" if I remember correctly.

Any-who, I got the hole dug and decided maybe a pop-tart would be a bit more my speed so I headed back to the house with my tools and a plan.

Teresa met me not long after in the kitchen to inform me that she intended to have a new freezer and I was to participate in its acquisition. A few "yes ma'ams" later and we were off on a two hour round trip to Watertown SD to purchase what seemed to be the only freezer left in the state.

Arriving in Watertown at the shop that had the freezer, we were informed that the employees were inside and the doors were locked but we could purchase our freezer and leave. There would be no shopping due to the apocalypse and all.

We agreed to their terms, exchanged a few shifty looks with the shopkeep and left within moments of arriving with our prize.

One would think this would make for a pretty full day... One would be wrong. We were just getting started.

After being eye raped by a skittish shopkeep like I was looking to steal his prize pig, Teresa decided we should purchase a weeping willow to plant for Annie the golden who we lost a few months back.

A little looking revealed a local plant and tree merchant (I later learned this is called a nursery, which is about to be proven extremely ironic) so we hauled tail that-a-way.

Once we were there and had located the willow trees on our own, I realized I was closer to an arsonist than an arborist and we were gonna need some professional help to pick the right tree.

Unfortunately, that help came with two young children attached (here comes the irony).

If ever there was a perfect contraceptive, these two little boys were it. Spend five minutes with these two little shits and if you still want kids, you deserve a medal or need medication yourself.

We held it together though. I didn't kick or bite or nothin. We got our help, the kids are still alive and annoying as hell and we were on our way shortly after.

An hour later and we were home at last, home at last.

Now the tree we bought was gonna need some immediate attention. As luck would have it, we paid enough for the tree, but we didn't get no dirt.

What we got was just a tree with some wet roots, so time was ticking and we needed to get this sucker in the ground.

Hannah and I got busy digging the second hole for the day. Luckily, the ground in that location was much more forgiving and we finished the digging in no time.

About twenty minutes later, we had ourselves a new weeping willow. Then it hit me... we forgot to put Annie's ashes in the hole with the tree before we buried it.

There was only one thing to do... I sent Hannah in the house to get Teresa and the ashes, said a few choice curse words, then set to digging the third hole of the day.

Tree planted, dog ashes buried, and freezer unloaded, now that's a full day right there... Except it's not!

I had a hole near the road that needed a mailbox planted in it. Since we were already planting things, Hannah and I decided to tie up that loose end too.

We no more than finished up and Teresa found a lead on a tractor nearby that we needed to go look at. We've been looking for a tractor since December and this was pretty close to just what we were after if the ad was to be believed.

So back in the truck we go and head down the road about 7 miles to check out this machine and determine if it's worthy of a place on the compound.

The couple who owned it turned out to be really nice folks which meant we chatted for longer than we should have; A few hours longer than we should have.

Ultimately, it turned out that machine was in fact a good fit for our place and we made an offer on it.

Our offer was accepted and we will have the tractor and accessories home this week. Stuff that was able to fit in the truck is home now as well as the box blade we purchased along with it.

After all that, the dogs are still alive (I checked), the cats are healthy and happy, Teresa and I are pooped, and I am just a few days from having my new farm throne home so I can play with a bit more horsepower.

If I move quickly, I can get me some bib overalls before it arrives and make this farmer title official.

And that my friends, is a full day!

YEAR OF THE PLAGUE DAY 118:

Today we were one with the land.

We worked the soil, improved the landscape, and brought some beauty to the compound.

In other words, we dug more damn holes! I'm starting to realize this whole farming thing is just digging holes and burying them again.

The day started by digging up a bunch of volunteer lilac bushes and transplanting them to a new location.

I took six good sized starters and planted them behind the wood shop to separate the shop from the grassy swampy area behind.

Teresa, seeing what was going on, decided to up the game and run to town for a whole crap load of new plants, shrubs, flowers, and the like to add to the landscape.

We got daisies, peonies, raspberry bushes, blueberry bushes, lilies, blue bouquetta, meadow sage, canadale gold wintercreeper, orange rocket barberries, and crimson pygmy dwarf japanese barberries.

Apparently, all those fancy names are parentals or perennials, or whatever means they come back every dagom year and we don't have to replant them all the time. Either way, that's a whole lotta holes.

Teresa and I divided and conquered. We transformed into human backhoes and farmed the shit outta this place. Every single plant, including the transplants got put into their new home.

Hell, I even got all of it watered, including the rhubarb after the planting was done.

As the day winded down, I start a list of projects in my head that I could accomplish when the new tractor arrives this week.

Project #1, figure out how to run the damn thing without killing my fool self or others. I'll let you know how that turns out as it progresses.

YEAR OF THE PLAGUE DAY 119:

I rubbed the sleep from my eyes this morning as I do most mornings and prepared myself for the 10 minutes of hunched over, stiff joint hobbling around required to get limbered up for the day.

As I looked to my right, expecting to see the clock reading about 6 AM, I realized something special had happened...

It's 7:15 AM and I did not get woken up by a whining dog wanting to test the limits of my no kill shelter policy.

Liberty the golden retriever actually let me get a full night sleep and I got to start the day on my own terms, not hers.

I'm a little ashamed at how grateful that made me. This dog really has it too easy but I'll take the win and be dagom grateful.

Once the blood was pumping and the joints were limber, I got right back to digging holes. We were able to do a bit of old fashion bartering with a local so I dug up some lilac shoots and traded even up for some raspberry shoots.

Our new raspberry bushes are now planted, watered, and ready to green up a dull area of the yard.

During all the back and forth in the garage today, I stumbled upon a new bottle opener. This bad boy is going in the wood shop.

Shaped like a pistol with a man and a woman in doggy style position, the bottle opener thrusts the man's hips forward each time you pull the trigger.

I'm doing my best to paint you a picture here but you won't be disappointed if you just go look for yourself in our facebook group...

https://www.facebook.com/groups/pandemicinthemidwest/

I don't know what the price tag was on this, but I can tell it's top shelf stuff, so I'll find a safe place for it and use it only for company.

After stashing the bottle opener in a safe place, it dawned on me that somewhere, there's a poor fucker whose job it is to paint the tip of the dick red on millions of bottle openers.

My guess is that this guy has an essential job that stays safe during the harshest of pandemics.

As the day began to wind down, we discovered that momma cat had indeed popped and had herself at least three kittens that we can see.

She's tucked into an old cat house without a way for us to get into it so Teresa used a selfie stick (two words that had completely different meanings in the 90s), to get a look at them with her phone.

We made her comfy and gave her some extra food and water and left her to do her momma cat stuff.

As post apocalyptic days go, this one turned out to be a pretty ok one.

YEAR OF THE PLAGUE DAY 120:

Remember the Simpsons cartoons where a devil sat on Homer's left shoulder and an angel sat on his right; all the while giving their best devil and angel advice and trying to persuade Homer to listen to them and not the other?

Today was that kind of day.

It started out well enough, most of the day was pretty well standard issue, and then came a text that changed everything.

The gentleman I purchased our tractor from could not get a trailer lined up for at least a few weeks. That meant I would have to wait two more weeks to get it home and that simply would not do.

I was informed that he had exhausted all his resources for a trailer and two weeks was really the best that could be done. So I did what any impatient new Farmville enthusiast would do… I started exhausting my own resources.

I made a few calls, sent a few texts, and waited a few minutes for replies. None of those replies were what I wanted to hear but one got me thinking.

I have this brother in law that tends to do his thinking in the emergency room AFTER he does something stupid but he is kinda handy and he's willing to try anything once.

I called him up and asked if he had a trailer or knew of one I could get, and the answer was the same... Nope.

He did however offer to just drive up here and drive the tractor home for me; it was only 9 or 10 miles from my house after all.

Knowing just enough about the tractor to get myself into trouble, I figured me driving it home was a pretty stupid idea. The angel on my right shoulder agreed.

It was only 9 or 10 miles though, and if It took me 13 days to get it home, I was still saving a day. Maybe driving it home myself is the right thing to do. The devil on my left shoulder agreed.

Round 1 went to the devil. I decided I was gonna roll the dice and take a nice long slow drive.

Here's the rub... There was still a large snow bucket that needed to be picked up with the tractor. I have the small trailer and I figured I could just use the tractor to lift the bucket onto the trailer and drive it home.

I of course assumed this, having no real knowledge of how to do such a thing but I was already rolling the dice, so there was no turning back.

Unfortunately, I can only drive one thing at a time (or so said the angel), so Teresa ended up having to drive the truck with a trailer.

She agreed that she could handle that so we set off on a mission sanctioned by the devil but supervised by the angel.

I'll spare you all the details of us idiots trying to pick up a bucket with a bucket and get it onto the trailer, suffice it to say, it was ugly but we made it happen.

And then the real adventure began...

Teresa set off driving my truck and trailer, flashers on, moving slowly and I got the tractor moving (forward after two tries) with flashers on, right behind her.

The angel appeared to be just as butt clenched as I was and was wide eyed, ghost white, and holding on. Not saying much at this point, I turned to see what the devil was up to.

The little bastard was relaxed, feet up, and looked almost bored. With a flick of his hand he motioned to the gear shift.

While trying to keep my eyes on the road and tearing due north at 2.6 miles per hour, I notice this bitch has a Hi, Low, and 1st, 2nd, 3rd, and 4th gears I can work my way through.

Now, currently I was in 2nd gear Hi, and after keeping things moving straight for the first ¼ mile stretch, I got a bit brave and decided I was gonna grab 3rd and put some road behind me. That's when the angel fainted, the devil laughed, and I pooped a little.

This ain't no four speed ford ranger, apparently, you pick a gear before you take off, you don't just grind through gears like Vin Diesel in fast and the furious. But not to worry, my first turn is coming up and I figured I could make adjustments after the turn.

As soon as I made the corner, I grabbed 3rd Hi, bumped the RPMs, and let the clutch out slowly. I ain't 100% but I'm pretty sure a few hairs on my head moved in the wind as I took off.

We were buzzing down the road going at least 3-4 miles per hour and this was getting real.

A few minutes down the road the angel tapped on my shoulder and let me know there was a car approaching from behind me.

I'm not sure how he managed to catch me at this break neck speed, but this car had no intentions of waiting behind me.

I bring the RPMs back a touch and hug the shoulder of the road. The car now had plenty of room to pass and proceeded to do so like a trained Nascar driver.

As long as I was slowed down, I pushed into 4th Hi. It was time to see what this girl could do.

The angel on the right was weeping and the devil was now finally paying attention. Judging by the blur of grass and fence posts that were flying by me, I estimated my speed at nearly 9 miles per hour and there was no hiding it... My knuckles were white, butt clenched, blood pumping, and I just passed a ground squirrel like it was standing still. (he was, he was standing still).

After what seemed like an hour, realizing later was probably closer to about 5 minutes, I saw Teresa ahead of me slowing to a stop on a bridge and a little blonde lady approaching the truck.

Keep in mind we just moved to this area. We literally know no one but here was Teresa being a social butterfly and making friends in the middle of a bridge on some back road.

I found out later at home that the little blonde lady was our old daycare lady from when our kids were tiny. How Teresa recognized her on a dirt road bridge fishing in a creek, an hour from where we knew her, I'll never know.

Regardless of the circumstances, I was happy for the momentary break. Slowing down, even for a few seconds, allowed me to try out a new move.

I continued to operate the complex machine while simultaneously waving in greeting as I passed the little blonde lady on the bridge.

Nailed it.

And THAT, was the first mile of our 10 mile drive.

Most of the remainder of the trip was uneventful. The devil tried to get me to push all that new horse power cross country a few times just to see what this thing could really do, but the angel won those battles and we kept it between the ditches all the way home.

Teresa pulled the truck and trailer into the yard and we did the whole ugly routine to get the bucket off the trailer and in its new home.

At the end of the day, the tractor was home, everyone lived, I believe the stains will wash out of my jeans, and I am ready to start learning more about my new yard toy.

YEAR OF THE PLAGUE DAY 121:

I was told once that when you own a tractor, half the time you spend with it will be fixing it. It appeared this one was no exception.

A few broken welds in really crappy spots could make this the first ever low rider tractor if I didn't get repairs made quickly.

I took the weight off the front wheels with the loader, and after a supply run to town for welding gas and other essentials, I repaired the welds and took the box scraper around the yard for the first time.

It's not as easy as they make it look on YouTube folks. I'll be leaving a few comments on those videos later. Apparently, a box scraper can become a box digger very quickly if used inappropriately.

So I dug some big holes and filled them back in for much of the last hour or two of daylight and called it a day.

Other than all that fun, today was pretty uneventful but I did get supplies that will help this weekend be more productive. I'm looking forward to learning how much I don't know in new and exciting ways.

YEAR OF THE PLAGUE DAY 122:

High hopes and expectations for today cycled through my dreams like an old View Master toy with unlimited slide wheels.

I had supplies, motivations, the beginnings of a plan, and daybreak had not come nearly as soon as I would have liked.

When the sun had finally made its way through the window in our room and I had dropped my legs over the edge of the bed in anticipation of starting the day, I knew something was not right.

An unfamiliar pain shot through my foot and I let out a barely audible but incredibly girlish squeak.

I looked down and noticed what looked like a zit on my toe.

Since I've seen almost everyone on Facebook lately is a doctor, I uploaded a photo for home care diagnostics.

I know, it doesn't look like much but let me tell you... this thing was painful and my whole foot was throbbing.

Even so, I got myself dressed and set out determined to get my day started.

I got the dogs fed, the cats fed, Remi got her meds, and I limped around the outbuildings like a landlocked, one legged pirate for the next half hour.

I even turned a pile of parts into a lawn sweeper in preparation for the yard being mowed today.

By the time I finished the assembly, my foot was killing me and I needed more coffee. As an added bonus, Teresa was now up so I had someone to whine to. The dogs didn't seem to give a hoot and the cats ran from me once the food was gone.

A few minutes of explaining my pain and Teresa had my foot up on the edge of the chair for closer inspection.

She gave it a thoughtful look, left for a moment, and returned with peroxide, a needle, a towel, and the look of a woman who meant me harm.

Once she was settled back in with my foot in her lap, she gave me the briefest of warnings and set right to work on it.

Jabbing it from two sides with a needle was enough to tighten the sphincter on the toughest fella, but when she squeezed from either side like she was trying to get the last of the toothpaste from the tube, I nearly lost my shit.

The gore that came from that tiny foot zit told me pretty quickly it was no zit. I cried a little, peed a tiny bit, and then breathed a sigh of relief as the pressure seemed to go away as soon as she was done and while it still hurt, it felt way better.

Now, with my foot on light duty but functional, It was time to get back to being a man and go outside where the women folk couldn't see me cry.

I gassed up the mowers and spent the next 3-4 hours being bounced around like I was on a hillbilly whip-a-whirl, that's a hardware store paint shaker for you fancy folks.

Hannah, not being one for rides, promptly disappeared as the work began and was not seen until later in the day when she was certain the coast was clear.

Teresa must have felt sorry for me because about half way through, I looked over and saw she had hitched up the 4wheeler and was using my new yard sweep to pick up the grass from the yard.

There's a few moments in a man's life when knows he got himself the right woman, Teresa squeezing puss from a foot injury and helping with the yard work may have been two of those moments in one day!

As we finished up, I expected her to give me one of those sarcastic "You're welcomes" and let me know how big of a favor she had done for me, which would have been unfortunate because I intended to have her tend my foot again later.

Instead, all I got from her on the way into the house is… "that 4wheeler needs a cruise control". Apparently holding that throttle at a steady speed while sweeping the yard was more challenging than she made it look.

By 1 or 2 PM we had the whole yard presentable and we went inside to rest up.

Truth be told, I rested, Teresa started painting her kitchen walls.

I remember her opening the paint, then everything went blurry for about an hour as I slipped into a coma.

Not long after I woke up, Danie, our oldest daughter, showed up to spend the weekend with us.

We always have fun when Danie and her husband Colin stay with us so I'm sure we'll find something entertaining to keep us all occupied over the weekend.

Maybe we could all take turns riding the hillbilly whip-a-whirl tomorrow.

Until next time, stay safe out there!

YEAR OF THE PLAGUE DAY 123:

Until today our little apocalyptic experience has been pretty peaceful at the Eckert Compound.

Today that ended and we have been attacked!!

It all started when I decided to get some weeds sprayed in key areas of the driveway.

These new Roundup bottles are self contained sprayers with a trigger, batteries, settings, and all kinds of confounding things that force a guy into reading instructions.

As I carried this complex jug of poison from the garage, I decided to use my tailgate as a bench and get to know the workings of my new tool.

I saw that tailgate being used as a bench part in a farm documentary and I had to try it out.

I approached the rear of my truck, opened the tailgate, and was immediately greeted by an angry wasp who we apparently locked under the bed cover the day before.

The little bugger was determined to put a stinger in me and I was playing harder to get than a prom date in the friend zone.

With my jug of poison still in one hand, I set off on a 50 yard sprint while limping on my one bad foot and I believed with all my heart that my time would have qualified me for an olympic tryout.

Long story short, the wasp missed but the declaration of war was loud and clear.

With no real regulation in the post apocalyptic world, I determined a short war was the way to go so chemical warfare was initiated and the war was won in a few short hours.

I believe there are pockets of resistance around the region but we are now on alert and our chemical stockpile is ready for deployment when needed.

Having secured a victory for the compound, Teresa and I got busy cleaning up the little barn and getting it ready for our new chicks coming in on the 11th.

As usual, Hannah disappeared as soon as the work started and managed to stay just out of earshot until both Teresa and I had our butts firmly planted in a chair for the day.

We moved some old straw along with a metric ton of cat crap from the barn but the cleanup was successful and we finally had a spot ready for the birds.

As the day wore on, my foot got more and more sore and red so

Teresa set me up for my very first virtual doctor appointment.

A quick hey, how ya doing via video chat and a picture of my toe was all he needed. "That's cellulitis" he said, to which I replied "does that mean I have fat feet"?

Apparently cellulitis and cellulite are NOT the same thing and he was not fat shaming my foot.

A quick soak a few times a day for my little piggies and some antibiotics is all I need to be back to normal and the whole appointment only took a few minutes.

So to sum up the lessons for today...

When fighting wasps, strike fast or run fast. (or hop fast in my case)

Teenage girls can sense work in the air like a shark senses blood in the water.

Doctors are not so bad when you don't have to go to them.

An old building can make a great chicken house if you clean out enough cat shit.

Until next time, stay safe out there!

YEAR OF THE PLAGUE DAY 124:

Quarantine has officially pushed us back into the years of old.

People are embracing a real little house on the prairie mentality and moms everywhere are turning into barbers and beauticians again.

Just last night our girls decided to get their hair trimmed by Teresa; some handled it better than others.

During Hannah's haircut I'm pretty sure I heard dinosaur noises coming from the kitchen. Fortunately, everyone survived and the haircuts turned out pretty well.

The morning rain set in, postponing all my outside plans, but not before mother nature gave us an atta-boy for all the hard work by way of new flowers budding all around us.

Heck, even my mild case of "fat foot" is feeling a bunch better today.

With the extra time on my hands, I found myself relaxing while watching the rain fall and tried to figure out why the hell Weird Al's song Amish Paradise is stuck on repeat in my head.

We are seeing some improvements on the quarantine front as Teresa was able to reschedule Hannah's dental appointments. FINALLY!

They do however require you to wear masks to come in. Teresa being the do-it-yourselfer decided that she would just whip up some face masks out of their socks.

She worried about their effectiveness until I told her they were FDA approved. I didn't tell her FDA in this case stands for "Fat Dads Association" but if I approve the mask and she feels better, I think this goes in the win column.

That said, we will go from Little House on the Prairie to the OK Corral in a hurry if she thinks I'm gonna wear one of those on my face.

Until next time... Stay safe, grow your hair out, and keep your socks on your feet!

YEAR OF THE PLAGUE DAY 125:

Y ou know what really gets my goat?...

That Cinco De Mayo would land on Taco Tuesday and you would not be allowed to gather with friends to celebrate because of a virus named after a Mexican beer.

Now that shit just ain't right!

But I wasn't gonna let that keep me down. In fact, even the steady cool rain wasn't gonna keep me bottled up today.

I decided to brave the weather so I started getting things ready for our first annual Midwest Redneck Triathlon in June.

It's basically a get together where true midwestern folk compete in traditional games such as cornhole, and horseshoes for a year worth of bragging rights and one killer homemade trophy.

Rain or shine, I decided to get some horseshoe pits done today so I could start training my body for the rigors of the upcoming events.

I know some of us aren't done playing hide and seek with this virus, but I have it on good authority that heat and an alcohol based sanitizer kills this little sucker. ** *medical disclaimer - I made this up, please don't take this as actual medical advice or share it as fact on your social media channels.* **

I think given there will be a massive fire pit, a few grills and a smoker going we are covered for heat.

There should also be enough alcohol to sanitize an ER so we can consider ourselves well armed with heat and alcohol sanitizer.

Someone call Trump and let him know the rednecks figured out how to sanitize the inside of the body.

All kidding aside, we still plan to hold the event on June 13th unless things change.

Most businesses including parks and such are opening up around here so we'll hold to our plans unless something changes.

Anywho, with the pits ready, I just need a load of sand and a clever way to keep the cats from using them as a litter box.

No one wants to toss horseshoes into cat poos.

Now back to Cinco De Mayo… I realize it's a Mexican holiday but just like we all turn a little Irish in March for St. Patrick's Day, we all get a little Mexican on Cinco De Mayo.

No, I don't mean we literally "Get a little Mexican", that would be wrong, I mean we all become a little Mexican in spirit.

We develop an accent and make fun of all the "Yeremys", "Yacobs", and "Yasons" we know.

We make inappropriate "Jalapeno on a stick" jokes and eat things that make us shit fire the next day.

This year will be no different on the Eckert compound.

In fact, Terrrrrrresa is whipping up some enchiladas and we do have some of the now famous Mexican beer on hand.

Take that Coronavirus!

Until next time, stay spicy out there!

YEAR OF THE PLAGUE DAY 126-127:

Every now and then a time comes when a man must tend his flock. The past two days have been mine.

We have a couple of young inexperienced barn cat moms who have been playing musical chairs with their kittens.

It's really no wonder since we have a few stray tom cats trying to get at the kittens around the clock.

To keep the new mothers from freezing the kittens by leaving them outside, and to keep the tom cats and other crazy mammals from eating the kittens, we decided to gather them up and seclude them.

With a few live traps baited with the smelliest of seafood flavored feline morsels, I placed them strategically around the property to catch the new moms.

Naturally, the first two cats I catch are a neutered male Hannah calls Spooky and another female we have taken to calling "Not the Dead One".

Not wanting to keep catching the same cats over and over, I decided to store these two goofballs in the air compressor room in one of the shops.

Both momma cats have been bedding down together and seemingly sharing the mom duties, so Teresa and I decided if we could catch one, we could get them isolated and move all the kittens in with that one until we got the other caught up.

Then, Teresa decided she was not waiting on my mad trapper skills so she walked up with my welding gloves on and snatched one of the momma cats up that was cornered in a box.

She just walked it right past me into the kennel we set up with that look on her face that's born of disappointment, mockery, and the satisfaction of a poor winner spiking the ball on their opponent.

I took a mental note that I will not be beaten twice and we got that momma cat who Hannah calls Titto (pronounced Tit-Oh), tucked in with all four kittens, a new litter box, food, water, and a bad attitude. I reset the traps for the night and day 126 came to an end.

Day 127 started for me at around 12:17AM.

Laying in bed I had a nagging feeling that something had taken up residence in one of my traps. I'm not sure how I knew, but if the psychic network could bottle that shit up I'd be rich because I was spot on.

After dragging myself from bed, half asleep, I grabbed a flashlight and stumbled outside to check the traps to see what kind of critter I had to deal with.

Unfortunately, I did NOT catch the other momma cat; all of a sudden they seemed to be playing shy.

Once caught, I'll have to remind them that if they had done that better a few months ago, we wouldn't be in this spot.

Still, my gut feeling was not wrong. There was something in each of my traps...

Two big, pissed off, stray tom cats. Unfortunately, we lost both toms to covid19 even after proper ventilation.

I spent the next 30 mins resetting the traps and doing my best to outthink the remaining momma cat. Once done, I went back to bed.

Near lunch time, I still had not caught this remaining momma that Hannah calls Patches, but Hannah and I did manage to put eyes on her. She was perched on the top of one of my tractor tires.

Growing weary of the war, I did what any great leader would do... I called Teresa out and handed her my welding gloves.

She had Patches in the kennel in short order. I packed up my traps, let the first two cats out of the compressor room, and we no longer speak of those events.

Until next time, stay humble or I'll send Teresa your way for a week.

YEAR OF THE PLAGUE DAY 128:

If yesterday was all about cats, today was dang sure all about the birds.

This morning, while overcooking my morning Poptart, I was greeted by a turkey wandering down the treeline and right up to our house.

Watching the turkey, I found myself having conflicting thoughts...

On one hand, that turkey would fit perfectly into my smoker and this guy right here likes him some smoked turkey.

On the other hand, the whole time I'm watching this giant bird work its way towards the house, it's eating its weight in ticks and other bugs in the grass.

In the end, my Poptart decided it. While the crust was a bit overdone, the warm berry flavored goop inside satisfied my hunger and I was able to let the bird get back to pest control and go on with my day.

Yesterday, before calling it a day, I found an old length of rebar and bent it into a real ghetto looking shepherds hook for Teresa's bird feeder.

By lunchtime today, that bird feeder was providing us with even more cheap entertainment in the form of several colorful hungry birds.

We all got to watch the birds for a few minutes before we hauled tail up north to Brookings to get Hannah's braces put on today.

While in Brookings, we made a side stop in Runnings and try as I might, I was unable to keep Teresa and Hannah from buying a few baby chicks before we left.

They tell me these are different than the ones we ordered. I guess these ones are layers so we can get a few eggs this year.

I went to Runnings for a yard cart that I could pull around without the 4wheeler and thanks to Teresa's obsession with chickens, I still don't have a cart!

Now I'm sure Teresa is going to tell you that none of that is true. She may take it so far as to say it was MY idea to get those chicks… DO NOT LISTEN TO HER. She can't be trusted.

Either way, I allowed the purchase of the chicks and while the girls call these our "layers", I call these our "practice chickens". We'll see how many of these we can keep alive until the other chicks arrive.

Until next time, keep your women folk happy, even if it means buying them chickens.

YEAR OF THE PLAGUE DAY 137:

Sometimes words are not needed... this is not one of those times.

It took a whole lotta adjectives to get this far with the new chicken coop, the new chicks, and a dog who is seemingly only alive to vex me.

On the bright side, there was progress, the coop is almost ready for birds, we have half a pork in the freezer (thanks Derek), and the new kittens are a week closer to rehoming age.

Hannah also finished all her school work for the year today so she can begin enjoying summer quarantine.

Teresa is still painting stuff, she may be painting stuff she already painted once at this point. I believe she is on autopilot.

As for me, I find it is now easier to buy hats than it is haircuts so I've moved one step closer to being a real farmer and taken to wearing a hat.

Until next time,

Tip your barber if you're lucky enough to still have one!

YEAR OF THE PLAGUE DAY 138:

Today we decided to take a trip to Harrisburg to tie up some loose ends in the area.

One of those loose ends was a visit to see my brother-in-law Matt and his wife Jenn so we could deliver a bag of long awaited, over priced fund raiser frozen meat.

Since we were already in the area, Teresa decided we needed to take a trip to Bomgaars because... well because that's just what farm folk do.

We did a walk-by of the chicken feed (something we probably could have used) and before long we found ourselves in the clothing department.

Long story short, this guy right here got himself some coveralls AND a new pair of boots!

For those of you who are on the fence about attending the Midwest Redneck Triathlon in June, maybe the attached photo will help get you to one side of that fence or the other.

I'm pretty sure Teresa approves as she's been smiling since she saw me in them. Then again, it could be a cringe but I'm a glass half full kinda guy so I'm sticking with it being a smile.

Anywho... Once home I had to try everything on and let me just tell ya, I felt dressed for success.

I felt the power of zero generations of farmers surge through me and knew I had to get outside and go straight to work.

I lifted a few heavy things, turned, twisted, fed some animals, checked on the bright eyed little kittens, and even took a knee a few times just to test the limits of my new wardrobe.

I was NOT disappointed. These suckers even have a pencil pocket and a place for a hammer!

Side note, they are a bit breezy but it may be user error. They did not come with instructions so I'm not sure if you are supposed to wear britches with them or not.

Either way, I think slipping into a new pair of coveralls must be the farmer's equivalent to staying at a Holiday Inn Express because I felt like I had a better handle on the land. I think I'll keep em.

Until next time,
Keep it classy folks.

YEAR OF THE PLAGUE DAY 222:

Today my daughter Danie and her husband Colin stayed with us and enjoyed a day of rural living.

As usual, morning came early on the farm and the dogs were napping as breakfast was being made for the lazy mongrels.

Even the cats were curled up on the porch sleeping in.

The remainder of our day Teresa and I shuffled the kids around the farm showing them all our hard work and introducing them to the animals like a kid showing his friends all his new toys.

The turkeys seemed happy to see someone other than my ugly mug and greeted everyone with a sideways stare and a gobble or two.

When the excitement wore off and the kids settled into their connected devices, Teresa and I did a bit more work on the new table top.

I was also relieved of my hat while Teresa washed it and set it out to dry. Apparently, my hat was filthy and smelled of "vinegar and ass".

Unsure of where I picked up either scent, I surrendered my hat and lived to fight another day.

Hannah fought off her boredom by making some kind of cloud bread. I think it smelled like eggs and felt like angel food cake.

Did you just gag a little? That was my reaction too.

As the evening wore on, our home was attacked by a few billion bugs out of nowhere. Our windows were COVERED in bugs like we had never seen before now.

Luckily, one of our recent auction purchases was made for just an invasion.

I dug some old swing set chain out of the junk pile and hung our new(ish) bug zapper and watched as the great bug extinction began.

I ain't gonna lie, I enjoyed the light show more than I should have.

Until next time,
Pick your battles and enjoy the small victories

YEAR OF THE PLAGUE DAY 143:

Today, another week closes and despite what the media says, the world still turns and we're all still here.

I'm still trimming trees and some days I think that's a losing battle. It is a pretty good workout though and my big ass needs that so I guess I'm winning the war.

If the South Dakota breeze ever calms down, we'll have a hell of a bonfire going.

One of the trees got a bit less trimming than the others because I didn't want to upset a nest of little sky steak chicks. For you city folk, sky steak is country speak for dove and they go great with cream of mushroom gravy in the fall.

Inside the home, I've started leaving flowers on the table for the girls so they know I'm still one of the good guys and they won't kill and eat me. It seems to be working so far so I'll keep it up.

The outdoor area of the chicken coop got some fencing today and a new gate.

Teresa thought we could do better on the gate so we spiced it up with some white pickets just for the hell of it.

By this time next week the egg laying chicks will be moving into the new coop and the meat birds will get an upgraded pen to finish growing in.

Last but not least, I got some new forks for the tractor this week so I can move pallets around. In fact, I got to move my first pallet from the driveway to the garage!

If this whole farmer thing doesn't work out, I may have a career in forklift driving.

Until next time,
Stay human.

YEAR OF THE PLAGUE DAY 153:

Our normally polite and gentle ladies were given leftover carrots and cucumbers today. It's the first time they have had leftovers and I wasn't sure what to expect.

Within moments, things turned fowl and a riot ensued. It was every chicken for herself as a feeding frenzy began and ended just as quickly as the veggies vanished.

Our group of meat birds looked on in stunned silence and disbelief. How could birds of a feather turn on each other so completely? Then I gave them food and they trampled each other like a bunch of idiots.

Across the yard just a stone's throw away, progress was being made on a new set of corn hole boards in preparation for the redneck triathlon.

Teresa got the horse shoes painted up, and finished a fresh coat of paint on the new benches as well.

On the north side of the property, a pack of wild kittens honed their killer instincts in preparation for being released back into the wild in 3-4 weeks.

When this happens, they will be introduced to our newest resident…

Charles (Chuck) wandered onto the property a few weeks ago and was skinny but super friendly. We gave him food, love, and the nod to take up residence in the area.

He then proceeded to thank us by spraying every vertical structure on the property.

We tossed him in a crate and he took a quick trip to the vet to have his nuts removed in order to get him back on track with the program.

Speaking of new residents, Hannah captured the neighborhood deer walking right up the driveway today.

Until next time,
Keep calm, 2020 is almost halfway over!

YEAR OF THE PLAGUE DAY 154:

Our new resident, Chuck, and our dogs have a love hate relationship and I may need to intervene before all sanity is lost.

Chuck sits on the window sill so he can watch TV with us from outside I guess. Who knows what this cat is thinking.

The dogs hate it and it results in a giant game of "I'm not touching you" through the window with the cat teasing and the dogs barking.

Not once since I've lived here have I wished for curtains on the windows but tonight they could save a life.

YEAR OF THE PLAGUE DAY 158:

This weekend we hit the city wide garage sales and we did pretty good!

We were really not prepared for a proper Christmas this past year in terms of decor, and with a bigger place, our little box of lights is just not going to do much.

$1 at a time we solved that issue today at the garage sales and we are much more prepared now. I believe my Christmas hero would be proud.

"When Santa squeezes his fat ass down that chimney, he's gonna find the jolliest bunch of assholes this side of the nuthouse" - Clark Griswald 1989

We also scored a set of Lincoln logs, new project bar stools for the kitchen, a few movie room posters, and a book of wisdom passed down over the ages of great men titled "Man Skills, The Complete Worst-Case Scenario Survival Handbook."

The girls were sure to point out one chapter titled "How to

Apologize When You Don't Know What You've Done Wrong" to me within minutes of returning to the vehicle.

We are now getting ready for the final week before the triathlon and on that note, we have our new smoker tested and ready to go and our 12ft banner showed up and is ready to hang.

I know 2020 has been hell on a lot of y'all, but as a fella who enjoys family time more than going out and enjoys being around crowds about as much as having a midget use my sack for a speed bag, I gotta tell ya, I'm not disappointed so far.

Until next time,

If you're like me, congrats on a great year so far…

If not, keep your head up, we could have flying monkeys this time next year.

YEAR OF THE PLAGUE DAY 161:

Before bed last night, I saw a social media post from my very own oldest child. The post is soliciting comments. If she gets 100 comments she says she will dump ice water on her father... me!

I ain't got much to say on that topic except that I now understand why farmers of old had large families. Every child after the 4th was a backup for when you needed to make an example of one.

On a brighter note, today I got the yard all mowed and the evening chores done just in time for the rain to start.

Since the rain was going to keep us fair weather farmers inside anyway, Teresa and I decided to make use of our indoor time to get some tables ready for the weekend events.

We finished off two tables in short order thanks to our super motivating mascot, Chuck, cheering us on. I'm pretty sure he's part amish.

We also dug up some JB Weld, beer bottle caps, green bean cans, mailbox numbers, and some sloth figurines from the dollar store to build some redneck triathlon trophies.

I ain't gonna say we are professional trophy makers, but they didn't turn out half bad.

Until next time,

Hug your children… but never turn your back on them!

YEAR OF THE PLAGUE DAY 166:

The morning began with a stiff breeze, a strong cup of coffee, and a can do attitude.

The animals were lounging, Colin my son-in-law and Teresa were preparing the meal for the day and I was raising the flag over the first annual Midwest Redneck Triathlon.

It wasn't long before rednecks from all over the land began pouring in to compete for the throne of Redneck Champion for a whole year.

Before we could get down to the brass tacks, teams were drawn and lunch was served. From pulled pork to gummy worm dessert, everything tasted fantastic and we all got the fuel we needed for the games.

Then it was on like Donkey Kong. Rednecks tossed horseshoes, bean bags, and giant dice in a race to the top.

All our teams fought bravely but alas there can be only ONE

team to claim the Midwest Redneck Triathlon championship.

In horseshoes, Matt and Janson won the bracket and scored a new roll of septic safe toilet paper.

On the dice, Jenn and Cole dominated the other rednecks and took a roll of tp back to their kin folk.

On the cornhole boards, once again Matt and Jason proved they were here to win and contrary to what their wives say, they can hit the hole.

Each individual win in each game not only moved a team forward in that bracket, it also scored them one point in the overall rankings.

At the end of the day, the team with the most wins was crowned our Midwest Redneck Triathlon Champions... Congratulations to Matt and Jason!

YEAR OF THE PLAGUE DAY 168:

s we recover from the events of the weekend we do our best to keep up with the rigors of farm life.

Sunday, we witnessed a cat we had not seen in a while, strut across the yard with 3-4 kittens following her.

Back in December we named this cat "Momma Cat" because she looked pregnant and we were feeling super creative. I guess we were right.

Later that afternoon I came face to face with one of momma cat's little killers. I retreated unscathed but the encounter reminded me we had work to do with our own litter of future mouse assassins.

Until now, we have kept our kittens in the shop to protect them and give them a good shot at survival. Most of them will be rehomed, but in the meantime they needed a place to stay that was NOT in my shop.

We decided to make them a new home where they could get

some much needed sunshine, get socialized with the local feline community, learn where their food would show up and when, and still keep them safe until they were big enough to release.

An old dog kennel, a cat house, and a few rolls of chicken wire later and I think we did an ok job of it. It must do a good job of holding teenagers too because Hannah spends a good chunk of her time there.

With everyone in their new home, we can now begin selection week and see who makes it onto the special Mickey Murder Squad and who goes to someone in need of lazy house cats.

Now that the cats are settled in, we had time to stop and smell the flowers.

Teresa is super excited because our very first "Grandma Joyce Flower" bloomed today. Daisies remind us of our beloved Grams so it was cool to see the first one of the year.

On the other side of the porch, a blue plastic flower bloomed and I found some sweet sweet nectar left over from the weekend! In other words, someone's blue cooler was left here full of beer from the prior day's events.

Until next time,
Step lightly around baby tigers and always check your coolers after a good weekend!

YEAR OF THE PLAGUE DAY 171:

Today began much like any other day....

I fed the dogs while my coffee brewed and then it was off to do the outdoor rounds while the dogs curled back up in bed with Teresa.

The cats get fed first, then a quick word with the turkeys, and finally the chickens get some fresh air and food for the day. That's the usual plan.

It wasn't until after exchanging words with the turkeys while they are still small enough to boss around that I noticed something about today that was different...

No wind. It was a calm and beautiful morning.

As I set off to take care of the chickens, I did so with a new outlook and a determination to enjoy my day no matter what.

Then I opened the chicken coop and those little fuc%*&# ... nope, I'm enjoying my day, chickens poop on things, that's just what they do.

With an adjusted attitude I finished my chores and headed back for the house.

On the way, I took the time to smell the flowers and admire the morning I had been blessed with.

Charles the cat met me on the porch where I enjoyed my coffee and his company before heading into the office to get some real work done.

But first... I took a picture of those flowers so I could help my daughters start their day with a smile and texted them off.

Then I picked a few flowers and delivered them to my loving wife and I was quickly swatted like a dog who just pissed on the floor for picking her flowers "like a dumbass" I believe is how it was put.

You can bet I'll be picking her some flowers from much further away from the house next time!

Anyway, half a day's work later, it was time to head into Sioux Falls so Hannah could visit with a friend who was visiting from out of state.

We dropped her off with her friends and then Teresa and I did some shopping. After which, Teresa asked me what I was hungry for so we could go eat before going back for Hannah.

Without much thought I said "a slice of lemon meringue pie and a coke". It's not much of a lunch but it sure sounded good for some reason.

We considered our options and headed to the only place we thought we could get such a strange lunch... Perkins.

We arrived and were seated in front of menus with a picture of a burger and a lemon meringue pie right on the front page... what are the odds.

As I flipped the menu open, the first (and I mean the very first) item was a combo with a burger, fries, lemon meringue pie, and a coke. Thank you baby Jesus for today!

Our waitress (a very nice young lady) takes our order and pretty soon a coke shows up followed not long after by a burger and fries.

For a Perkins burger, I was pretty impressed. The meal was better than I expected and I was anxious to get to dessert.

Our chipper little waitress showed back up and asked if we would like to get started with our pie order and with a giddy smile of anticipation I said, "We sure are!"

"Lemon Meringue," I blurted out like I just won the special olympics and could not contain my delight.

"Ahhh," she said "We're actually out of lemon meringue, I'm so sorry."

I'll admit, my heart sank a bit but Teresa and I had already been talking about this pie menu and I had narrowed down a close second before we even ordered our burgers.

With a bit less enthusiasm I delivered my backup order... "I guess I'll take the banana cream", I told our waitress.

"Like hell you will" is what I heard come back to me but I believe what she actually said was, "I'm so sorry, we're out of that too".

I now dislike this girl.

Maybe it was her tone or maybe it was the fact that I could clearly see the smile in her eyes even though a mask hid her real smile.

Just like the chickens earlier in the day, she was shitting on all the nice things.

I looked at Teresa in time to see her openly smiling like a six year old who just won a cake walk. She was loving this!

Then I remembered my earlier vow to enjoy my day. I relaxed my grip on my butter knife and ordered the coconut creme with a look that dared her to tell me it was out as well.

Then Teresa made her order, which they had first try of course, and we waited as our waitress with a mean streak headed to the kitchen to tell her coven about the fat guy she made cry.

By the time she returned, I had regained my composure and announced that I was looking forward to enjoying my lemon meringue pie.

Teresa looked at me like I finally lost it but I made it clear, coconut it might be but in my mind this was the best lemon meringue pie and that was just that.

She scoffed, I enjoyed my faux lemon pie, and we left Perkins with just as much of a smile as we entered with.

We headed home shortly after so I could spend what was left of this beautiful day getting the yard mowed (some of it anyway).

Until next time,
Make lemonade, even when life REFUSES to give you lemons.

YEAR OF THE PLAGUE DAY 172:

I've stubbed enough toes to know life is a balance, everything has its day in the sun as well as its day in the shitter. Balance, karma, call it what you will.

Yesterday's peace and beauty were balanced out today in what will forever be known as the Canton Slaughter.

Morning chores were finished up and with our little homestead taken care of, we jumped in the Chevy and headed south once more.

Beyond the big city of Sioux Falls near a town called Canton that was first settled in 1867, lies a cozy little acreage where Matt and Jenn call home. This was our destination.

As we pulled into my brother-in-law's place, there was an ominous look to the sky. It was 9AM but nearly dark from storm clouds, seemingly over just Matt's property.

And then it began to rain. A straight down, big drop, drench your ass to the bone rain for about two straight hours.

Luckily, South Dakota folks are a hardy folk and we were not gonna let a little rain slow the plans for the day.

Within minutes of arriving, the local residents and outside help were working in unison to begin the bloody sport of processing chickens.

Jobs were divided up based on skill level.

A young man named Landon was sent to catch the chickens because he was quick on his feet and short enough to avoid bumping his head on the low roofed chicken run.

He snatched them up and delivered them to the murder cone were they were allowed a moment for last words, last rights, and then SNIP. A quick killing cut with the proper redneck chicken chopper, otherwise known as tree pruning shears.

A few minutes later they were dunked in a scorching pot to loosen the feathers and then it was off to the chicken tickler for plucking.

This little machine is amazing. It takes a chicken from feathered to naked as a Vegas stripper in less than a minute and it shoots the feathers right out the bottom into a bucket for easy cleanup.

Teresa felt most comfortable manning the chicken tickler. I think it's because it looks like a washing machine but I didn't tell her that while all the knives were sitting around.

Next the chickens went to mad man Matt where they were eviscerated, violated, waterboarded, and stuffed in a cooler of ice. There was a lot going on and in a few short hours the slaughter was over and the cleanup was under way.

If not for this accounting of the day, no one would know of the horror these chickens faced.

In honor of the fallen, #WhiteMeatMatters, I picked up some gas station chicken strips on our way home.

Until next time,
If your shoes are not blood stained, thank your local butcher.

YEAR OF THE PLAGUE DAY 175:

Today I spent equal parts of my day in the yard, in the machine shop, and in the chicken coop.

I guess the machine shop comes first since my day started there.

While doing chores in the morning, one of my traps was sprung and as luck would have it, inside was a cat we have never been able to catch, until now.

Her name is "Britney Bitch." There's a story there but we'll save that for another day.

As with all the cats we catch, they go for a ride to the vet to be spayed or neutered and then spend the night in the machine shop to recover before being released.

However, before we ran to the vet, I needed to finish up the chores so I took her to the shop to wait in the shade.

The turkeys are also in the shop and as I opened the door to take the cat in and take care of the turkeys, the no good orange cat we call Charles walked right out of the shop like he owned the place.

I have no idea how he got in there but I know he spent the night there and I know our turkeys probably had an encounter with him.

Sure enough, the wire on top of the turkey enclosure was pushed down, the water was dumped over and the turkeys were as flighty as a millennial with a job offer.

Luckily, they were all alive, just a bit shaken.

It did shine a light on another issue though; these turkeys were going to need a better home sooner rather than later.

Enough about the birds for now though. With morning chores finished up I made a quick trip to the vet's office to drop off our latest catch.

Instead of leaving her to be spayed, the vet brought her right back to me and informed me that this cat is 1-2 weeks at most from giving birth to a new litter and they could do nothing with her just yet.

Lucky me!

So back home I went and spent a while in the shop building a new enclosure for this dagom cat to have her litter in.

I'll be danged if I'm releasing her back into the wild because I know I'll never catch this one again and she'll drop another litter on my steps in a few months.

With Teresa's help we got her settled in with fresh food, water, litter, and straw bedding. Now we watch and wait.

That's all I got to say about the shop.

Next, it was time to spend some time in the yard.

With the great weather lately, most of our swampy wet areas in the yard have dried up. Even the southern shelterbelt is back on dry land.

It's gonna take some doing, but I hope to have it all reclaimed soon.

The main yard even dried up enough to get the tractor out and start knocking down the mini race track the previous owner left me. (not even kidding, there is an oval go-kart track in the yard!)

I guess I figure a redneck triathlon every year is more than enough, we don't need a Nascar track in the yard so it's time to class the place up a little and get it out of here.

It will take a lot of dirt work but I should be able to level a lot out and get some low spots fixed at the same time if the weather holds.

Since I'm tearing up the main yard, I can at least take solace in the fact that the rest of the yard is still looking good. The daisies are in full bloom, we have our very first lily, and I discovered a mulberry bush while mowing!

While I was working in the yard, Hannah was packing up a

few hundred boxes to be shipped out for work. Teresa gave her the task for some extra spending money but I don't think she counted on Hannah getting it done so quickly.

I also discovered a new dash ornament in my truck left by my girls because they think they are funny. It's a tiny little yellow windup chicken.

The trick is on them though, I love it and the little guy will have a name soon.

And that brings us to the chicken coop.

While taking a short break in the house and talking about God knows what with Hannah, I noticed what looked like a chicken walking free outside our chicken coop.

Hannah and I took off out the door to investigate and sure enough, we had a free bird roaming around and nine other birds being harassed by the damn cat Charles.

I'm pretty sure he was someone's house cat and they dumped him and I'm starting to get it. Maybe he got kicked out because he's a bit of an ass hat to have around.

Either way, Hannah grabbed a stick and entered the chicken run like a momma bear defending her cubs.

I didn't see Charles enter the chicken coop, but I'd be willing to bet he looked a lot more graceful going in then he did going out.

Shortly after that, Hannah and I had the escaped chicken back with its friends and the girls were perched up off the ground for a much needed breather.

The whole ordeal did get me thinking...

I fucking hate that cat, our turkeys need a new home, and these chickens did pretty good staying alive with an attacking cat in the coop.

I decided there and then to add on to our chicken coop and move the turkeys over. Maybe the chickens could help keep the cats away.

I added an additional 7ft to the inside coop with a divider to keep the chickens and turkeys separate for now but keep them close enough to socialize for a while before we combine them.

It turned out pretty good and the turkeys seem to be loving the extra room to roam.

The build itself was pretty uneventful, but about half way through, I heard the chickens making a hell of a fuss outside again.

I looked through the small window into the run and our cat Spooky was getting overhauled by one of the chickens.

The best way to describe the scene below in the chicken run was to say it looked like a strange rodeo where chickens rode cats.

Try as he may, Spooky could not shake that chicken and by the time he exited the chicken run I'm pretty certain he had no desire to tangle with a chicken ever again.

That ought to just about do it for today.

Until next time,

We are now giving away kittens and selling attack chickens to all interested parties.

YEAR OF THE PLAGUE DAY 177:

Today I was determined to rid my yard of the go-kart track once and for all. I knew I was in for a lot of tractor work but I was committed to the task.

Once I finished my day to day stuff I saddled up 72 horses worth of red hot diesel power and got to work.

Sure it's the first real job I've taken on with a tractor but YouTube showed me all I needed to know so I dug in with the confidence of a 5 year old boy in a batman costume.

Dig, push, drag, repeat. On and on it went for at least two hours. Getting the steep track banks cut down with the loader felt a lot like breaking up concrete with a spoon but I did get it accomplished.

When I felt like the high parts were knocked down enough, I hooked up the box blade and started dragging over the track Over and Over and Over to break it down even more and level out some of the dirt.

This part went on for another couple hours until the sky started to cloud up on me.

By this time the heat coming off the tractor had cooked my feet, my ass was getting blistered from bouncing around the tractor seat, and my mouth was as dry as a popcorn fart.

It was quitting time and I was thankful for it. Almost as thankful as I was when I found out the girls had done all the evening chores for me before I parked the tractor.

I believe if we don't get too much rain I can finish up with the box blade in another hour or two and then clean up with a drag section.

For future reference, this shit was way easier on Farmville.

Until next time,
May your yards grow green and may you never need to remove a race track from them

YEAR OF THE PLAGUE DAY 183:

Sunday, the misses and I made a flying trip to Omaha to drop the girls off with Danie.

It was a really quick trip and I wish we could have spent more time but farm life called us back home.

To be more accurate, fat helpless chickens and turkeys who needed food and water called us back home.

Even with Hannah gone for the week, her wilderness training keeps on giving. She set a few traps before leaving and as luck would have it, Monday morning bright and early I had a skunk to deal with!

We had a viking funeral for the skunk and my trap is on the far side of the property until next year when I hope I can get within 10 ft of it again.

Not to be outdone, her cat Charles took over rabbit population control duties and it looks like he can handle the job well enough.

For doing such a good job, he was rewarded with a little leftover meatloaf. He followed that up with a six hour food coma.

The next morning, her remaining trap was inhabited by a little grey kitten whose curiosity got the better of her.

She'll be fed, spayed, and taken care of for a few days before turning her loose again to go find her litter mates.

Speaking of kittens, we've been able to rehome a few of our kittens but we have four left as of today. We'll be working hard to pawn them off to loving homes in the coming days.

"Britney Bitch" also popped and had 4 kittens… two orange, one black, and one calico. We'll be looking for new homes for these ones as well in about 7 weeks.

It's starting to feel like a cat nursery around here but we have spayed or neutered every damn feline on the property that we have been able to get our hands on. Next year should produce a much smaller crop of kittens.

I was also able to find a few drag sections and with enough WD40 and wrenching I am slowly turning a few scraps into one decent drag section to start leveling the yard out and breaking up the clumps from the old go-kart track.

And finally, did I mention we have Free Kittens ready for new homes?? Tell your friends!

Until next time,
Listen to Bob Barker and spay and neuter your pets!

YEAR OF THE PLAGUE DAY 185:

Happy 4th of July Eve to America and all her inhabitants. May you all enjoy your independence day and may 2020 chill the F*$% out for a day so you can!

As we prepare for our own 4th of July celebration, Teresa has taken over the kitten whispering since Hannah has been away.

In just a few days she took the new little grey kitten from a hissing, psychopath to a little purr box who loves tummy rubs. After the 4th she can go in to get fixed.

The living chicken strips are getting super fat and will be ready for murder day on the 5th. I'm looking forward to not cleaning out a chicken coop every other day; those girls shit more than is natural.

On a positive note, I got a break from the smell of chicken crap for a few days thanks to Petunia the skunk coming to visit. Variety really is the spice of life.

Finally, just in time for the 4th, I was able to get one good drag section built from the scraps I brought home and it works pretty well!

The yard is ready for rain and grass seed and maybe this time next year I'll have a decent looking yard again.

Until Next Time,
Enjoy life's chicken crap, some day it may be skunks instead.

YEAR OF THE PLAGUE DAY 187:

Today was a full day. Made more so by the fact that last night was a sleepless night.

I seem to have the most patriotic neighbors in America. Porta-Potties, Fireworks, Grills, Campers all over the property, these folks were settled in to celebrate their independence right.

A flash of light followed by a boom like thunder followed by the drunken howl of 20 odd rednecks. That was the scene on repeat last night until shortly after 2:30AM

I almost couldn't help but cheer along with them between booms. They committed so completely that the cheer was infectious.

I did resist though, mostly for fear of what Teresa would think of me if I woke her up clapping and jeering like a retard at 2AM.

The next thing I remember it was 6:30AM and I was getting ready to start preparations for the day.

Today was chicken chopping day, the day the last of our kittens were leaving, the day our momma cats were being released after being fixed, the day our kitten Tinsel would be moved to her new two week home, and the day Hannah was coming back home.

There was a lot to prepare for!

7:15AM - feed and water all the animals. Spend an extra 10 mins doing it because everyone needed to be talked to like they were orphaned children.

8:00AM - Mow the yard around the house and the strip near the lean-to where we would be working. Make vroom vroom sounds because it makes the mower faster in my mind.

8:30AM - Use the trimmer on the lawn around the house so it's pretty for momma when she gets up.

9:00AM - Get Teresa moving so we can get to town and get the few supplies we still need.

9:15AM - Get the chicken chopping station setup.

9:30AM - Circle back around to make sure Teresa was mobile and make a list of what we need.

10:00AM - Hit town for some light shopping with Teresa. We were a little ahead of schedule at this point so we bought ourselves a new lawn ornament!

When we returned home, Teresa took the house and I took the yard and we ate the snake from both ends. Before long I was ready to fire up the boiler for the birds and Teresa had the house ready for company and the grill ready for lunch.

By noon people started to arrive. First was Matt and Jenn, then Brian and Hailey, then Colin and Danie, then Heather and Austin. It was a full house before we knew it.

And so it began... We were chopping up chickens like a fine tuned machine. For anyone considering raising meat birds, I highly recommend butchering your brother-in-laws flock first, it made ours go quite smoothly.

With a short pause to see off our remaining kittens to their new owners, we powered through the chickens quickly and before long we were taking a lunch break while all the birds cooled in the coolers.

Hannah helped get our two kittens settled into their new 2 week home in preparation for when we release them for the final time.

We wrapped up the day by packing the freezer and coming inside for some homemade strawberry rhubarb crisp.

I'll sleep easier tonight knowing I have 22 chickens in the freezer to help tide me over during the apocalypse of 2020.

As I'm finishing up with this post, behind me a rainbow ushers the day out as if to say, you sir are one blessed SOB.

Until next time,
Thank you to all who helped and/or cheered us on.

YEAR OF THE PLAGUE DAY 203:

It's been a few weeks since my last entry and while my life is generally boring by any standard, I did learn a few things over the past few weeks that I believe are worth passing on to further generations.

#1: I learned that people are desperate for entertainment - I was informed at the family reunion that many of you actually read this drivel (I won't hold it against you but I think you can do better).

#2: I learned I'm a big softy for a sad face - I discovered that after being fixed, Liberty can REALLY turn on the puppy dog eyes and get pretty much whatever she wants. I also learned later that dog shit in the backseat of a Chevy Malibu on a 90 degree day is less fun than it sounds.

#3: I learned I have a future in chicken training - I found out that even if my ducks are not in a row, my chickens lineup nicely. Especially when putting the cats on notice about who rules the porch.

#4: I learned sometimes you wish life would give you lemons - Apparently when you save cats, the word gets around and "cat adjacent" creatures start showing up. This is skunk number 3 to find itself in my yard and on the pyre this summer. It's not lemons, that's for dang sure.

#5: I learned that the girls are working against me - Teresa and Hannah will go to any length to nurse a sick kitten back to health so we can deal with the little turd later.

#6: I learned a handy man is only handy to have while they are being handy - Teresa provided another stack of wood and a pile of work from some evil son of a bitch on pinterest. Guess I'll be building a kitchen table and a coat rack soon.

#7: I learned gravel driveways need to be maintained - Seriously, who knew. I figured a bit of gravel and grading once in a while but this driveway wants to grow weeds now. I sprayed it all down with salt water today, I'll let ya know how that turns out.

#8: I learned that rewards come to those who work hard - I put a lot of hours into the yard on a bouncy old beat up cub cadet but today I was able to trade up to a new machine. Teresa gave the thumbs up on a new John Deere so I must have done something right.

#9: I learned that turkeys have personality - One of our turkeys has formed a habit of perching on its water can each morning so I can pet it before I leave the run. It's odd to be sure and I know you should not play with your food but this goofy little fella just loves a good head scratch. He's now named Chris (short for Christmas).

#10: I learned one final lesson... Never eat a late supper of Taco John's and then head to bed. I nearly shat my own sheets folks. Taco John's WILL NOT hold overnight. That's a quick turn around food. Fast food in every sense of the word.

I think that about gets us all caught up. Until next time,

Pet your turkey, it might just make ya smile!

YEAR OF THE PLAGUE DAY 208:

This week our nephew Matthew came to stay with us and help out around the place. An extra set of hands is always welcome!

We met his parents halfway in Wessington Springs to pick him up and we had an opportunity to snap a picture of the road just outside of springs that our son Brian was born on. (yes, he was born in a Dodge Neon on the side of the road).

Anywho... after stopping for ice cream and getting home, we settled in for the night and everyone hit the sack. In the morning, Matt's introduction to farm life began.

First thing in the morning, Matt was ready to roll so he could go see the kitten JoeJoe. This is the cat we tried to talk his folks into taking home and he still seems to have some attachment to her.

JoeJoe doesn't seem to mind the extra attention and they keep each other busy.

After I got him peeled off the cat, we made a quick round doing chores and headed off for the first auction we've been to in a VERY long time.

We had two items picked out ahead of time that I was interested in, we were determined to stick around until those items were sold and then head back home.

As Eckert luck would have it, one of the items was not going to work for me so I took it off the list and the other was destined to be sold late in the day. That means we got to stick around for all the little stuff and bake away in the hot sun for 3-4hrs.

It wasn't a total waste of time though, I grabbed a few good deals and the rest of the time we acted like tourists and took pictures, did some bird watching, and I'm guessing we provided some much needed entertainment for the real farm folks at the auction.

On a side note, having Matt with you at an auction is like playing poker in a house of mirrors.

I'd quietly tell Teresa, "That item looks good, we can bid up to $20 on it". Five minutes later the auctioneer would be close to selling that item and Matt would loudly announce, "You want that right!? You said you'd spend $20".

About then, the old farmer next to me would chuckle and smile at me with his Copenhagen stained John Deere t-shirt with the sleeves cut off.

We were playing with a handicap for sure but I was still hopeful and it was time for the item I came for... A drill press with some dents and dings but in pretty good shape.

I had a talk with Matt about playing close to the vest before we made it to this part of the auction and he was playing it cool.

The auctioneer slapped a few flattering adjectives on it to make it seem like a diamond in the rough and then jumped right to the business of selling it.

35, 30, 30, 35, 40… This is going well I thought.

40, do I have 45, 40, Up my hand goes, placing my $40 bid and feeling good knowing I'm still well under my set budget.

Then in the blink of an eye this fast talking auctioneer pulls in eight more bidders driving the price from $40 to $130 and well beyond my budget. The auctioneer had these farm folk in the palm of his hand and worked up into a bidding frenzy.

Now I know why old school mobs had pitch forks; they were farmers all riled up from some damn auction.

I give the auctioneer a side eye and he returns my look with a grin that says better luck next time chubby fella.

Well played sir, well played.

That was it for our auction experience. We were all hot, tired, and ready to put some distance between ourselves and this auction.

We got home, cooled off, ate some grub and called it a night to close out the first full day of Matt's stay with us.

CORY ECKERT

Until next time,
never trust an auctioneer.

YEAR OF THE PLAGUE DAY 209:

Sunday morning I sounded the wakeup alarm for Matt at about 7:20AM. I ain't gonna swear to it in a court of law but a curse word may have slipped past his lips when that bedroom light came on.

Nonetheless, he rallied, splashed some water on his face, and was ready to take on the day just a few minutes later.

So far having Matt around is a lot like watching an episode of Scooby Doo when Scrappy was with him. What he lacks in size or ability he more than makes up for in blind confidence and enthusiasm.

We made quick work of the normal chores and then turned our attention to a few things that needed a bit more attention.

First, we cleaned out the chicken coop and the turkey coop. It's a dirty job but he didn't blink. He dove right in and got things done. **Mike Rowe** would have been proud.

Sure the wheelbarrow is bigger than he is and probably outweighs him by a few pounds, but that didn't stop him. He emptied the coops quickly and was excited for the next task.

We broke up a new straw bale for fresh bedding, rinsed and replaced the water cans, and had the coops looking like new and all the while Matt was making new friends with the birds.

I believe he was motivated by the promise of getting to hold and pet the birds when he was done. Luckily, the birds did not disappoint and were all too happy to accept his attention. He even found a favorite chicken he likes to hold when he does chores.

Next we did a little yard cleanup with the loader. Before we were finished, Matt had me running the pedals while he ran the wheel and the hydraulics for the loader. I believe if he was another 4inches taller he could have done the job himself.

That was all we had time for in the morning. Matt has a standing appointment to watch a daily youtube video release. 12-1PM is a time where Matt disappears into his room to enjoy his daily soap opera.

From what I gather, he watches a grown adult have fun playing video games. I guess this is just what the kids are doing these days. Damn you Covid for changing the entertainment world so much!

After relaxing and cooling off for a bit, we got back to doing things "IRL", that's "in real life" for all us old folks who are not up on our internet slang.

Teresa finished up her garage sale bar stool salvage project, Matt and I set a few traps out to clear out some smelly critters, and Matt made friends with the newest generation of mousers.

Hannah and Matt even took a ride on the 4wheeler while Teresa and I were working in the wood shop for a bit (no that's not slang for anything, we really were working).

As the evening wore down, Matt and the girls tried out a snack box from Russia with goodies such as salmon and cheese flavored chips with tartar sauce dip included.

When Matt is not being entertained, you can find him outside trying to cuddle with the kittens. Mom and dad will need to check his bags when he leaves or he may smuggle one home with him.

That's it for day two of the Matt Adventures.

Until next time,
Keep your coop clean and buy your snacks local. Sorry Russia, yall eat some nasty shit over there.

YEAR OF THE PLAGUE DAY 210:

Yesterday was a Monday much like any other Monday I suppose. Morning chores went by quickly and breakfast was underway, then from the other room I hear Hannah and Matt talking about Old Yeller.

Naturally my interest was perked, so I started listening a little more closely as I went on with my work. It turns out, Matt read about Old Yeller but had never seen the original movie.

So back to 1957 we go! I turned on the film and went back to work and the house was super quiet (other than the TV) for the next two hours.

I peaked out a few times and didn't see any tears but if I was a betting man, I'd say they were there!

With that off his bucket list, we had a few errands to run and getting the boy a haircut was top of the list.

He and I ducked our heads into every hair place in town until we found one with some time to fit us in. They were half good haircuts at a half good price but we both walked away with a bit less hair and that was the goal.

For those of you with a few kids, you may understand the aggravation of the words "I'm bored". Shortly after returning home from haircuts, Matt started hitting me with this little phrase.

Three minutes later, we had a shovel in the boys hands and he and I were filling holes the dog dug in the backyard.

It's really hard to be bored when you are trying to fill holes in a fenced yard while keeping the dogs in the fence and simultaneously trying not to step in dog shit.

We were both hot and sweaty by the time we finished and with boredom beat, he was ready to retire to the air conditioned house for a while.

Just as we sat down, the dogs delivered our reward for all the hard work. Since we did such a great job filling holes for the dogs, the dogs decided to bring some of that dirt inside to level out the carpet.

Teresa was impressed as you may imagine.

We lounged around for the next few hours but when evening chore time approached, it was Matt's time to shine. The bird chores were all his and he did not disappoint. We may have a bird whisperer on our hands.

He had the chickens and the turkeys fed, watered, and tucked in for bed in no time flat.

Steaks on the grill, Ice Cream for dessert, and Shrek the Musical to close out the night. I don't know about y'all, but i'm not sure it gets much better than this.

Until next time,

Stay entertained, and if you are looking for a digging dog I have one for rent.

P.S. our crazy cat Charles showed up after 8 days missing. wonder how long he'll stick around this time.

YEAR OF THE PLAGUE DAY 211:

It may come as a surprise to some of the young ones but there really is a season for everything and those seasons go by in the blink of an eye.

Which is why I was completely caught off guard when I realized my "cool uncle" season had grown cold and I was gonna have to step up my game to keep my street cred with Matt.

Lucky for me, Brandi gave us some inside information about Matt liking Pokemon cards so I recruited Teresa to take the boy to town and hunt for some.

The hunt was successful and I had bought myself at least one more day as the "cool uncle". Take that Father Time!

This cleared my calendar for the morning as he sorted and re-sorted his new found cards at least half a dozen times.

As he enjoyed his victory, I plotted the best way to use the new found good will and squeeze some child labor out of the boy after lunch.

I had just the project, we needed a new bench for the kitchen and with the help of a few fart jokes and life lessons I figured I could drag the project out until dinner time and finish the day out without a single moment of boredom.

I could see in his eyes a few times that I came close to losing him. The glassy eyed look of disinterest would start sneaking in and I'd snatch his attention by handing him a power tool.

Sure enough, that would bring him back to life for at least another few minutes. The bottle of glue may have kept him the most entertained and engaged of all his tasks today but a win is a win in my book.

Three hours... we stretched the assembly of half a dozen chunks of wood into a three hour project in which we both stayed entertained.

In a world of instant gratification and quick results, it was nice to savor the process as much as the result for a change and I now have a reminder of Mathew each time I sit down and get a sliver in my ass.

Matt and I were on such a high from our accomplishments, we even gave the dog a pedicure before dinner!

Until next time,
Enjoy your small victories and allow the pains in your ass to remind you of better days.

YEAR OF THE PLAGUE DAY 212:

Trigger Warning: Animals were harmed in the making of this documentary

The days with Matt have grown long and I am not the fountain of energy I once was so I let him sleep in today until 7:45AM.

We both stumbled through our wake up routines, me getting coffee, him wiping sleep from his eyes asking why chickens need breakfast so early.

As I took my first sip of coffee and looked out the window to see what kind of day we were walking into I noticed something out of place near the far tree grove.

A few days back Matt set his traps there and it looked like one was rolled over into the yard.

Matt and I grabbed the binoculars and squinted through the cheap lenses that are narrowly better than my phone's camera zoom and we could tell that trap was definitely NOT where we left it.

Sleep left his eyes in an instant and he beat me to the door by a good ten feet. We got through the chores in record time thanks to his new motivation and then it was time to go check traps up close.

We got to the first trap and it looks like it got rolled around the yard by a bear. The bait was gone and it was at least twenty feet from the trees laying on its side.

Down the tree-line I could see our other trap was sprung but from our angle we had no idea what kind of creature was in it.

If you've ever been sprayed by a skunk, you would fully understand the caution and side stepping manner in which we approached the second trap.

In a half moon arch we circled the trap and got ourselves a better vantage point and then we saw him, a big ole raccoon in Matt's trap and only a dozen or so yards from the chicken coop.

There was no point in approaching closer until we could deal with him properly so we headed to the house to grab the rifle.

On the way back out, Matt had a dozen questions about our options. Knowing he had just watched Old Yeller get put down the day before, I put it as gently as I could but made it quite clear, this critter was about to be ventilated and pronounced dead of covid.

We said our goodbyes, gave him a quick death and a warrior's funeral on a wooden pyre while reciting the Chicken Lives Matter motto.

With the fire burning, we turned our attention to cleaning up the traps so we could reset them later.

In hindsight, giving the boy control of the water hose may have been a mistake. We both saw more water than the traps did before he finished.

After lunch Matt and I decided to get the pellet gun sighted in. We noticed the scope was way off the first day he was here so we set up a target and stepped off 50 yards.

Unfortunately, Matt tried and tried but his arms were too short to hold the gun and he was unable to do much with it. We did get it close enough for rabbit work and put it away for later.

We finished the day off with a game of catch and a trip to DQ drive through for ice cream. It turns out, I eat ice cream better than I throw a football.

Until next time,
Be thankful when your flock is safe but prepared to defend it when it's not.

Oh, and if you're over 40, throw a ball once a year so you don't make a fool of yourself when the skill is required again.

YEAR OF THE PLAGUE DAY 213:

Today wrapped up the final full day of having Matt with us. It was a day of cleanup and relaxation for the most part.

Even so, there are always a few extra life lessons you can squeeze into a young mind.

Yesterday Matt asked when our garbage truck came to get the trash. Today he got to experience the burn barrel and the smell of burned garbage; I think he prefers the garbage truck.

While the garbage burned down, Matt tried to sneak a few extra loves out of the cats but most of them were not having it.

After lunch, we made the local birds happy by refilling the feeders. We also got to see evidence that birds had finally moved into our new birdhouse.

This was all followed by a lot of sitting around and watching TV. Tomorrow, we return the boy to his family and hope that his experience was a memorable one. Failing that, we hope we didn't damage his outlook on life too much.

Until next time,
Only the lord knows how many of us will survive this plague, treat every moment as either a teaching moment or a learning moment.

YEAR OF THE PLAGUE DAY 216:

After taking the weekend off to go camping and return my nephew Matt back to his parents, we were right back into the swing of things this morning.

Today the turkeys would be introduced to a whole new world. It's time for them to earn their keep by getting rid of small critters, ticks, bugs, and some weeds so it's free range from here on out.

After a few encounters with the curious cats, the pecking order had been established and the turkeys were comfortably exploring their new found freedom.

We were proud parents to be sure, we even celebrated with some free range chicken wings (the turkey's neighbors for a while) to mark the occasion.

But they were not the only ones reaching a milestone at the Eckert ranch today.

The new litter of kittens graduated from their indoor only nursery to the indoor / outdoor kennel. They now have a lot more room to run around and get used to being outdoors in case they end up being farm cats.

The move was not without incident though, Teresa being super NOT cautious decided the best way to move the mom cat was to just grab on and walk her out. Teresa was wrong.

The momma cat latched onto Teresa's finger like a fat kid with a ham sandwich and did not want to let go.

A few high pitched screeches later we tossed the cat into a kennel (the proper way to transport her) and relocated her to the new home.

Teresa played with the kittens for a little longer and then retreated to the house to doctor her wounds and curse the momma cat out of earshot of her kittens.

Until next time,
Remember that freedom comes at a cost, but it can taste amazing and goes well with ranch dressing!

YEAR OF THE PLAGUE DAY 219:

You know how the military does war games every so often to hone their skills, build teamwork, and stay on top of their game? Teresa and I do the same from time to time to keep our marriage strong.

This time, our war games consisted of locking ourselves in the wood shop and trying to complete a project together.

We were armed with sharp objects, blunt instruments, power tools, and any manner of wicked devices. The mission... build a kitchen table as a team, without killing one another.

There were a few muffled curse words and an icy glare or three but we finished the day just hours from having a new kitchen table and completing our mission.

We are now waiting for glue to dry overnight and we can finish up with a bunch of sanding, staining, and sealing. We also got the bench Matt and I made sanded and stained.

While we were hard at work in the shop, the turkeys and chickens had taken over the yard. Oh, and birds have caught on to where the cats get fed and now eat all the cat food before the cats do, so there's that to deal with.

I sure do miss the days when farming was more about digging holes than dealing with critters.

Speaking of critters, after working hard in the shop, we rewarded ourselves with some cuddle time. The three little rodent assassins from the latest (and hopefully last for a long time) litter of cats, are pretty cute and I'm not ashamed to admit it.

They will still be leaving just as soon as they are weaned and able to. Cute don't buy the cat kibble after all.

We have Sherman, the orange cat with a white face and white socks. Sherman is a boy, the largest of the bunch, and is super cute but more cowardly lion than lion king.

Next we have the other boy Jack. Jack is the smallest but is the first to the food bowl and the first on your lap for love. He's just brave enough to make a great little night time assassin some day.

And finally we have Cali. Cali is a girl named Cali because we jumped to the conclusion that she was calico. We found out later that her coloring is actually tortoise shell but the name had already stuck.

Until next time,
Marry someone you can trust with a saw and do your research before naming things!

P.S. Does anyone know if birds are still free range if they eat cat food? Asking for a friend.

YEAR OF THE PLAGUE DAY 221:

Today we turned a surprise birthday party into an opportunity.

Jenn invited us to celebrate Matt's birthday and part of that celebration would include playing cornhole.

It's not everyday you get to train with a redneck triathlon champion so we jumped at the chance.

I ain't got a lot to say about the quality of training except there's a reason you should never meet your heroes. The rest of the day was a hit though.

The party had all the essential pieces to be a success. Walking tacos, cake, cold drinks, and good company.

The girls got some much needed gossip time and the guys shot some stuff and discussed important world events.

Just as the atmosphere was starting to feel a little upscale, Matt walks around the corner of the old Chevy pickup with a pair of nunchucks.

Believe it or not, those nunchucks took a group of adults through fourty five minutes of conversation ranging form home defence to sex swings and I only wish I was kidding about that.

Matt displayed his skills with the weapon and within moments smacked himself in the face with his own nunchucks. If I'm being honest, I think we all saw it coming well ahead of time.

After that, folks started leaving little by little. Some to head home, some to pick up a buck to breed sheep, and some to find more sophisticated conversation.

All in all, the day was a good day, we even took the opportunity to visit Jenn's chickens while we were there so we could swap poultry parenting advice.

Until next time,
Never meet your heroes and hide your nunchucks to avoid awkward questions.

YEAR OF THE PLAGUE DAY 224:

Today we celebrate Teresa's birthday.

Being the good husband I am, I got chores done early so I could make her breakfast in bed.

My culinary skills were tested but the presentation made up for any lack in cooking ability.

Today she enjoyed a pair of poptarts. One third perfect, one third burned, and one third cold, because our toaster has consistency issues.

But I set my mind to making her a good breakfast in bed and that's just what she was gonna get so I garnished those pop tarts with a Little Debbie oatmeal cream pie and served them on a paper plate with a bottle of Diet Coke.

After breakfast was finished I gave Teresa her birthday gift... a few hours without me pestering her!

I walked the property like I was Lewis and Clark exploring the Louisiana Purchase. I discovered what I thought was a cherry tree but was informed later is a wild plum tree and I even found another mulberry tree on the far side of the property.

The trees don't appear to be in great health but I'll see what I can do about that as soon as I find out where I left my green thumb.

During my expedition, much like Lewis and Clark, I faced some dangerous wildlife.

There were a variety of large ferocious cats, the largest of the cats weighed in at nearly a pound and a half and had eyes that just followed you like a fat guy watching the ice cream truck.

There was also a spider that I'm pretty sure was part grizzly. This thing looked like it could pull down a buffalo and I wasn't getting any closer to it than I had to.

After my walk and a few hours of mowing, Teresa fed us BLT's and we jumped in the car to go get ice cream.

With our ice cream in hand, Teresa decided to take a sunday drive around town on a tuesday.

It was a beautiful day for it and since we were still exploring, we were still running into wildlife. We had to pull over and let a group of wild turkeys cross the road.

Teresa and Hannah were oohhing and ahhing as at least a year's worth of turkey jerky waddled across the road free for the taking.

I reminded myself it was Teresa's birthday and blood would not be spilled today and we slowly wandered home and called it a day.

Until next time,
Every now and then, be a tourist in your own yard. You might be

surprised what you find!

YEAR OF THE PLAGUE DAY 226:

I'm not overly superstitious, and I don't really buy into the whole Friday the 13th stuff, but from this day forward, I will forever be cautious of Thursday the 13th.

After our first few days of free ranging the turkeys, I decided to confine them to the run because, well… they like to run.

Herding turkeys back from your neighbors land is nothing like the old westerns where sturdy men herd longhorn cattle or wild horses. There is absolutely no way possible to look cool herding a flock of turkeys even if you are wearing spurs.

That said, today for some reason I was feeling generous. I let the turkeys free to get some fresh grass and bugs and told myself I could rely on their thankfulness and goodwill to return them back to the coop that evening.

Shut up, it's not funny!

Anyway, that went as well as you're imagining and that's all I have to say about that.

The chickens on the other hand are developing skills I was unaware they could develop.

The largest of our girls took over the protector role after riding our black cat from one side of the run to the other after he tried to introduce himself.

If professional sports do not come back soon, I would highly recommend cat and chicken rodeos. The entertainment value is way up there and I pay the athletes in grain. (they do occasionally shit on stuff)

But I digress... back to the skills...

We named this big boned chicken protector Bertha and today she started crowing like a rooster. I had no idea hens could do this but Bertha wasn't into labels so she is doing her own thing.

She sounds a bit funny but I wasn't gonna tell her that on her first day of real practice. You be you Bertha!

Then mid morning arrived and the sun was warming the place up. I was willing myself out of my chair to get my second cup of coffee when I saw movement out the window.

It was small and clear across the yard but I definitely saw movement.

I scrambled to find my binoculars and steadied myself on the window to get a look at what creature I was gonna have to deal with.

Fully prepared to see yet another skunk waddling across the yard, I was surprised when it was actually a snapping turtle about a foot long.

I booted up and went to get a closer look but after a brief introduction and me explaining a few ground rules, I let him go on his way untouched.

It wasn't until later I realized, I just had a conversation with a turtle in my front yard.

At this point in my day, there are signs that mental health may be a concern if the pandemic goes on too much longer, but I have no time for that kind of thinking.

I had work to get done in the office but I was struggling to make it happen.

Liberty, our golden retriever, was doing everything in her power to be the center of attention and since my office is the only office upstairs, I get to enjoy her antics while Teresa works in peace.

But I'm a problem solver and this was just another puzzle to be solved.

I knew Liberty had a pet peeve. She can't stand it when things outside change. If the view outside our front windows change in any way she loses her shit.

Next time I left the house, I placed a wheelbarrow out front. As soon as she gets used to it, I change it up and put something else out there.

She's now glued to the window wondering what kind of sorcery is turning her world upside down and I am able to work in peace for at least a few hours.

Until next time,
Never judge a hen by its crow and use your enemies weakness to your advantage.

YEAR OF THE PLAGUE DAY 227:

Life is full of humbling moments that keep you guessing.

For example, this year alone we have wrongly assumed the sex of at least four animals on our little farm. To make it worse, we named them ALL.

Joe (the tiger king) cat turned out to be Josephine while his/her sidekick Carol(the baskin) turned out to be a Carlos.

That may have been the start of our misnaming adventures but it surely would not be the last of them.

Ginger, our orange cat who plays super hard to get is actually more of a Garfield. And our latest oops, Bertha the chicken turned out to be Bubba the chicken.

Today we make reparations to those still with us and give our heartfelt apologies. We are also debating whether or not Bubba becomes chicken and dumpling soup next week or if we really want a rooster around.

Until next time,

CORY ECKERT

There may or may not be something to this "gender is fluid" thing but one thing is for sure... I ain't the guy to ask!

YEAR OF THE PLAGUE DAY 228:

I've had mixed feelings about our turkeys lately but I woke up this morning determined to bend them to my will.

I ain't sure if turkey training is even a thing but today it was. We started with a few slow walks around the inside of the run.

Slowly we graduated to outside the run and before long, we were taking walks around the property with me taking on the role of head mother clucker and eight trained turkeys following me around.

I know I'm too old to win a 4H ribbon but I may look into getting an honorary one for my work with these girls. They are nearly pleasant to be around now!

Once my turkey training was finished, it was time to get on with the day.

In every great farmer's life comes a day where he finds himself standing in front of an auctioneer at a livestock auction.

Some handle the experience with grace while others are scarred so deeply they look for 9-5 work and leave farming in the past.

I ain't sure where we fall on that spectrum but I'll do my best to recapture the details of today and you can decide for yourself...

As Teresa and I pull up to the auction house we exchange looks and a few judgemental comments about how small it looks.

We were expecting something bigger from all the talk we heard from the locals. Either way, we were committed so we parked the truck and started our tour of the grounds.

Before we made it far, my brother-in-law Matt and his son Landen showed up and we exchanged greetings then continued our tour as a party of four.

There were all sorts of exotic birds, majestic stallions (AKA: miniature ponies), a single donkey, a few types of goats, cows, and even a pen full of llama's.

And that's just the animals. Inside the auction house there was a dimly lit cafe that smelled of grease and health department violations.

As we entered, I did a pocket check to ensure I still had my wallet and then surveyed the room... I counted fourteen people, twelve teeth, and a case of code red mountain dew.

Two of these folks were young men with full on joe dirt mullets, sleeveless button up shirts, and skinny jeans with fade marks where a can of skoal rested.

I'm pretty sure one of em caught me staring but I couldn't help it! I did my best to recover and fit in with the small, unique ecosystem of people gathered in the room.

I'm not sure if I was feeling brave or trying to prove I was "one of them", but I ordered some homemade banana cream pie and a coke.

Now I'm not the kind of guy to eat gas station sushi but this has to be right up there in the risk reward category.

While I ate my sketchy pie (it was actually pretty good), and the others with me took bets on my future bathroom visits, Teresa acquired a bidding number for us.

The auctioneer spoke over a PA system to let us know they were beginning the auction outside with the hay so we wrapped things up and exited the way we entered.

I had no interest in the hay but there was a small stack of straw bales I had my eye on so we posted up near them and waited for the auctioneer to work his way to us.

As I'm waiting I hear the girl behind me chastising her father. She couldn't have been more than eight or nine years old but she was letting him have it.

I believe the words that finally moved his feet where... "Dad, there are llamas here and you wanna sit here and look at dead grass?"

It was a well formed question and it must have worked because off they went towards the barn to pet the llamas leaving me with only a few guys to compete with for the straw bales.

Unfortunately, a few guys were all it took. I had a top dollar cut off of $3.50 per bale because I knew a place to get them for $4 per bale.

These particular bales sold for $5.50 per bale!

Oh well, it was a small loss and we could now go inside and settle into the bleachers for the live stuff. Teresa even took the time to get a selfie of the four of us just before the bidding started.

As the auction for a pair of guineas began, I overheard the old farmer behind me tell his buddy that he was quite disgusted with his own guineas because they are loud, worthless, ugly birds.

I take my wisdom where I can find it so I took guineas off the list of birds we might want.

About this time in the day, one of the auction hands pointed out a mistake the auctioneer made and the auctioneer asked loudly over the pa if he would like to come up and do the sale.

An awkward silence followed as the fella weighed his options and ultimately decided to let it go and keep his job for the day.

There was still a little tension in the air so I figured I'd make my way to the restroom while the room collected it's composure again.

I located the run down unisex bathroom in short order. I grabbed the knob, turned it, pushed the door, and looked 250lbs of redneck woman directly in the eye.

You gotta believe me, I wanted that door shut again, and fast, but I was shocked into standing still just long enough for her to pull her young son in front of her and say, "I'll be just another minute sir".

I looked behind me into the crowded cafe and saw a few heads shaking and a few hidden smiles. I could almost feel them planning the ceremony to marry me off to ole Becky Joe because I had seen too much.

True to her word, just a minute or so later she exits the restroom and I'm able to escape the disapproving stares.

I entered the bathroom and did my best to complete my business while holding one arm outstretched to the door just enough to catch it if it was to open.

I wasn't sure if there were hardware issues or if Becky Joe was just super friendly but I wasn't taking chances.

Once finished, I cast my eyes to the floor and walked back through the cafe and into the auction barn to find my seat again.

I had seen things I couldn't unsee, but my spirit had not been broken. I just needed something to lighten the mood up.

I think that's why I raised my hand and bid on two cute little ducks. To my surprise, I won the little ducks and they were our first purchase of the day. Take that Becky!

Not to be outdone, Teresa bought herself a box of chickens that were brown to "get some more color in the flock".

When she realized she won the bidding war against someone else who wanted that box of chicks, she got all smiley and announced, "that was kind of a rush!".

Nope, give me that number woman. Calm it down. Teresa went into a timeout for a few minutes to get her bidding adrenaline back in check.

Next to us, a lady is buying up a full flock of birds at a time. The girl with her asked, "what did you just buy in that box?". To which she replied, "I'm not sure but they were cheap".

Now that I think about it, that's about the time I saw Matt head to the restroom. (I did warn him about Becky).

As luck would have it, Matt avoided Becky only to pull the curtains back on another poor woman trying to do her business.

Someone needed to speak with the owner about buying a cheap lock! This bathroom was like a giant game of redneck roulette.

After this, Teresa and Matt started coordinating bathroom visits via text and left a guardian outside the room. I believe Matt even stood guard for me once.

At the end of the day, the auction was a pretty fun event and we came home with ten new birds. We paid a total of $1.90 per bird so I think we did ok.

Now we just have to figure out what they all are!

We have two unidentified ducks, two birds that I ain't sure if they are even chickens, and six brown/red chickens to "add color to the flock".

We got them home, I cleaned out the turkey coop and evicted my newly trained turkeys, and set them up with a new home to get acquainted with the rest of the flock before mixing them together.

To make sure Matt didn't go back home to his wife empty handed, I caught up one of our black chickens and sent it home with him.

That leaves me with a few minutes to rest and then head back out to build new roosts for the turkeys before bedtime.

And THAT is how our first livestock auction went.

Until next time,
Knock twice, knock hard.

YEAR OF THE PLAGUE DAY 231:

Late last night Teresa and I discovered we had one very unhappy turkey.

It turns out, the turkeys got too fat for their perches and all eight turkeys no longer fit. That left one turkey on the ground in a foul mood.

We quickly formed a plan to extend the perch and I set off in the dark to gather tools and materials. Teresa stayed in the run with the turkeys and the flashlight to console the distraught bird.

Before long, we had a workable perch and we tucked in our future holiday meals and headed to bed ourselves.

This morning, I left the house after just a few sips of coffee and did my best to make up for our poor poultry parenting by spoiling the girls.

The turkeys and the chickens got a swing installed from an old broken down swing set we found in the trees. If that don't make em happy, I'll arrange a day at the gravy spa for the complainers.

Later in the day, Teresa and Hannah said farewell to our three remaining kittens as they left for new forever homes.

Hannah started setting an ambush right away to catch the momma cat so she can go in and be fixed in the morning.

That should conclude our cat farming responsibilities for 2020 and we can now turn our attention to more important farming tasks.

The first of which was finishing the new kitchen table and bench seat.

We're pretty proud of how it turned out but I'd be lying if I said it was easy. My wife curses like a sailor folks and she's a strict taskmaster.

With the help of Hannah, Teresa and I got the old table out and the new table and bench into the house and set in place.

Within hours, I was staring at a pickup full of new lumber and was informed that new kitchen chairs were now on my todo list as well as a few other projects.

Has any farmer ever seen the end of a honey do list? Asking for a friend.

Until next time,
Never lend your wife your truck unless you have free time on your hands.

YEAR OF THE PLAGUE DAY 233:

Yesterday I decided it was time to upgrade the turkey run once again.

I was informed that turkeys like to rooste higher off the ground and I also wanted to build them some type of wind break before the cold weather hits.

After a few hours of searching the property for scraps I could use on the project, I was able to enclose the top of the north facing part of their run.

It wasn't pretty but it's functional and sometimes good enough is all you're gonna get so I set my sights on the finishing touches... a new perch.

I grabbed the chainsaw and fell a tree that had been needing to come down so I could use a large branch as the new turkey perch.

A few chops of the saw and the girls had a place to get up off the ground and out of the wind.

Before calling it a night, I checked on the birds and all but a few had found a new spot on the branch and were happy as a turkey can be.

It was time for a good night of sleep for me but I was unable to sleep well after walking in on Teresa sitting in bed with a charcoal mask on.

I'm not sure this is the political climate to be selling blackface beauty products to white girls but I'm no politician so I could be wrong.

Even the golden retriever Liberty was looking at me like I had answers as to what the hell was going on with her face.

Sadly I had no answers and the dog and I would both get a restless night of sleep filled with horror movie thoughts.

One good thing came from it... I was ready to be out of bed super early this morning so I had chores done and slapped a coat of paint on the new addition all before the girls got out of bed.

I even caught Hannah before school and forced her to take some "first day of school photos" because I know how much kids love doing that.

Then she masked up like a bank robbing nurse and drove off as her mother and I waved from the front window.

Until next time,
The Eckert farm has a new policy, If you're wearing a mask on my property, I'll assume you are a bandit.

YEAR OF THE PLAGUE DAY 233(AND A HALF):

One entry for today just didn't feel like enough so I've added a bonus entry!

It dawned on Teresa and I that with the cats all rehomed, we had a little empty nest syndrome going on and we needed to fill that nest back up.

With some expert advice from youtube and a half assed plan, i devised a way to fill the nest and my stomach at the same time!

Meat Goats!!!

Hannah had been saying she wants goats since we moved here, I like eating things, and Teresa loves kids of all kinds.

By lunch time, it seemed to me I had nailed this plan so completely that there was no turning back. I had talked myself into it.

But first, I had to clean out the back side of the barn and get a pen ready for some new inhabitants.

It was a dirty job, one I underestimated greatly, but one I finished in record time. I even dug up some lumber from the lower half of the barn to make a goat pen. The plan was coming together.

When I finished, Teresa and I did some looking around and before long we found two or three farms with the kind of goats we were after. (the tasty kind)

We exchanged a few texts and calls and before long we were on the road to adopt a few new kids for the farm.

We pulled into the goat farm and as soon as we exited the truck, we heard what sounded like an infant being beat with a stick.

Around the corner walks a husky fella holding a little reddish colored goat that was screaming its ever lovin head off.

We exchanged pleasantries, agreed to his price, and informed him we were looking for two goats to take home.

He turned around and marched into the goat pens while still saying words to me about which goats I wanted.

I say he was "saying words to me", because I have no idea what the crap he was saying. I thought he might be having a tourettes episode but I played along and shook my head yes while saying "yep", alot.

It wasn't until we were on our way home and Teresa was looking up "keeping goats alive for dummies" that some of those words started to make sense.

It turns out, black belt, dapple, and red are all color patterns in this breed of goat but here's something to think about goat people...

Normal humans don't use those words in normal conversation and without some foreknowledge, you may find yourself looking over your shoulder at someone like me with a confused, glazed over look on their face.

That said, we did wrangle two young goats out of the pen and asked the fella for any advice he might have for newbies about raising goats.
I think he actually laughed as he walked away but I ain't one to shy away from a challenge so off we went, heading home with goats in the back.

Once back home, we settled the new girls in just in time to surprise Hannah after she returned home from work.

We tried to fool her with the old, "go grab my hammer" redirection but she ain't no dummy so mom had to tell her to "shut your pie hole and grab the hammer". Then she saw them.

As I finish writing this entry, Teresa and I are inside and Hannah is still out in the barn with the girls trying to think of names.

Until next time,
Whoever said you can't eat your problems was just plain ole wrong.

YEAR OF THE PLAGUE DAY 234:

6:05 AM. That's as long as I could keep myself in bed today knowing there were two new residents that might not be 100% comfortable yet.

We had a lot of work to do and it wasn't gonna do itself so I got an early start on chores.

I knew as soon as I stepped outside we were in for a miserable day of work. Even at 6:15AM it was humid and starting to get sticky.

Humid enough that a salamander actually crossed the yard right in front of me!

I cursed my luck but finished the chores just the same. With the chores done, I made a list of materials I needed from town so Teresa and I could make a quick morning trip.

We made quick work of our town errands and then it was time for the stop I had been waiting for... Runnings had bird feed for the turkeys and food and water pails for the goats.

They also carry lots of miscellaneous man stuff like my brand spanking new pliers and leather holster!

I gotta tell ya ladies, short of a well made sandwich, a trip to Runnings might be the best gift you can give a man.

But the fun can't go on all day so we hightailed it home so we could get to the work of the day.

We had a fence to put up that would serve dual purpose for the goats and the turkeys to do some grazing.

The fencing is electric netting and looks like it would be super simple to put up, it was not. It's actually a considerable amount of work to get the fencing up, bury a ground rod, run hot and ground wires, and hang and connect the energizer.

All this was made that much more difficult in the 80% humidity and 94 degree heat.

Within ten minutes, Teresa and I were soaked to the bone and struggling to keep our pants up thanks to the extra weight of sweat.

Normally I wouldn't have an issue with this but as millions of inner city kids can attest to, it's a real son of a biscuit to get anything done with your pants halfway down your ass.

We worked through it though, because that's just what South Dakota folks do.

We also cursed at each other, complained, and over exaggerated our discomfort at every opportunity because that's just what South Dakota folks do.

By the time we were finished, the task had pert-neart killed us, but we were far from done for the day.

Our new residents needed a bit more food and bedding so we made arrangements to pick up alfalfa and straw bales.

Unfortunately, the alfalfa bales were about forty five minutes south of our house and the straw bales were fifteen minutes north.

That's the bad news, the good news is the truck has AC and a soft seat and both those things sounded pretty dang good.

We set up pickup times with the owners of the hay and straw and hit the road. About two hours later all the hay and straw were sitting in the shed at home and we were in sight of the end of the day.

Hannah on the other hand was NOT ready to call it quits. She was determined to make friends with the new goats who are still nameless as of this entry.

She's doing pretty good too! These little meat sacks would scream bloody murder if you tried to touch them just twenty four hours ago and now Hannah has them eating out of her hand.

I approve of her making them comfy and asked her only to make sure she names them after food so she has an easier time eating them later.

I believe she is calling the black and white one Oreo now.

Until next time,
Sleep when it's hot, work when it's cool, and don't let your kids play with their food.

YEAR OF THE PLAGUE DAY 237:

The past few days have been a roller coaster of work, exhaustion, feelings of accomplishment, and moments of defeat.

Bringing the goats home a few days back tipped off a chain reaction of jobs that needed to be done and at the time of writing this, I see no end in sight.

The weather is still hotter than a louisiana hemorrhoid and breathing the air is like being waterboarded but we did what we could to push through.

The first order of business was getting a new hole cut in the wall of the barn so the goats could get in and out.

My plan was solid, until the hole was actually in the wall. Then the holes in my plan became apparent real quick.

It turns out, if goats can exit a hole, turkeys can enter that same hole. It also turns out, a few stall gates hold goats really well but they don't hold turkeys worth a damn.

I now had a real problem and I was alone since the girls were off on a road trip.

Turkeys were boiling over the gates in the barn and goats were testing my new electric fence outside and I had absolutely no control over either situation.

I slammed the door to the barn behind me to keep the turkeys inside. This also cut off what little light comes into the barn so I was fighting eight 10lb winged demons in the dark of a small barn.

I made a few hoops and whoops and kept about half of them on the ground in the stall and started wrangling the rest in corners and chucking them in one at a time.

Once all eight were in the stall I tossed some old gates and other junk on top of the stall to hold them in temporarily.

The whole thing took about five minutes but it felt like twenty and once again I have to question the decision making that led to having turkeys here.

But what's done is done. I had turkeys in the goat stall and goats in the turkey run but at least everything was somewhat secure so I could solve the next issue... How to keep turkeys out of the goat stall.

A few minutes of kicking junk around and I had some old eighteen wheeler mud flaps cut to size and hanging over the door opening.

My thinking is that a goat can be trained to push her way in but a turkey ain't got the real estate in its caboose to push through.

It has been a few days now and so far that theory holds water.

I even built the goats a little step out front so they could enter and exit from about the same height.

The rest of the day was spent cleaning out behind the barn so I could start my next big project. The whole area was about three feet high in weeds and full of old telephone poles.

With the help of the trusty old farm tractor I was able to chain and drag out one pole at a time into the front yard.

Teresa was pretty pleased with me when she saw that mess but I convinced her it was all part of the master plan and she seemed to believe me.

After thinking about what that master plan was for a day, I set off this morning to start implementing it the best way I knew how... blindly and with enthusiasm.

Here's the plan... I'm gonna use the chainsaw like a lumberjack and cut those poles into usable lumber for my next building project.

Here's what actually happened... I spent four hours on Youtube learning how to use a chainsaw properly and researching the best way to get 4x4s out of telephone poles.

Once i was filled with misplaced confidence, I got to work.

Unfortunately, I ain't no lumberjack and no amount of Youtube is gonna fix that. After about four hours of work, I accomplished the following things...

Cut two log saddles to hold my work in place, used the loader to place a pole into the saddles, measure and mark my first cuts, and get Teresa to help me run a chalk line on my marks.

I got about half way through the first cut on one side of the log before my saw got real hot. I let it cool for a bit and when I started the saw back up the chain would not move.

I tore that saw down into pieces and reassembled it twice, gassed it back up, added bar oil, tried again and still no movement in the chain.
Then I learn an important lesson... always check the chain brake. This lesson was driven home by the laughter of the woman who "says" she loves me.

We did finally make it through the first cut before the rain moved in and the sun set on us.

Well, I made it through the cut, Teresa killed buggs with a hammer as I cut the pole.

At this rate, I'll have a usable 4x4 in about two more weeks.

We did get to end the evening by watching our ducks play in the water bowl. If that doesn't put a smile on your face to end the day you might be a little dead inside.

Until next time,
Sometimes ideas sound better on paper. When in doubt, watch some ducks swim and think about it some more.

YEAR OF THE PLAGUE DAY 239:

Today I forced myself to complete a project I have been dreading... cutting telephone poles into enough posts for my new project.

After the first cut, I was sure this task would be in my eulogy but I started it and I was determined to finish it.

I got my chainsaw blade sharpened at Ace over lunch and after work I was out of excuses to put it off so I got back at it.

A sharp blade, fresh gas, and new bar oil for the saw had it running tip top today and it gave me way less trouble.

That said, the pole was still solid as granite and each cut was nearly thirty feet long and a foot deep.

Just before sunset I had finished making my required eight usable posts.

In the process, I learned a few things about myself.

1 - If I ever need to rely on my lumberjack skills to build shelter

for my family, we are probably gonna die.

2 - I have way more stamina in my head than I do in reality.
3 - My tree grove was the home to a very large porcupine who is now deceased having been hit by a truck near the end of the driveway.

Until next time,
The Eckert sawmill is now closed for business and reopening does not look promising.

YEAR OF THE PLAGUE DAY 241:

There's something special about a Friday that lifts the spirit of any workin man. Maybe that's why I woke up with a good feeling about today.

Teresa and I did some cleanup in the outbuildings and made room for all the vehicles including the camper to be parked inside.

It seems like such a small thing but it's the first time the shops have been clean enough to park in since we moved here so it sure felt good.

We could have called it a day right there and it would have been a pretty decent day, but I knew Friday wasn't done with me.

Back inside I was settled into my office chair when my oldest, Danielle, sends me a message asking if I could "photoshop a pit stain out of a photograph".

I don't want yall to think this is normal, I swear to little baby Jesus, no one in my life has asked me to do this before.

That said, she's my little girl even if she is twenty three, so I told her "sure i'll give it a shot".

I guess she knew I could handle laundry in photoshop better than I do in the washing machine because I had her looking cool as a cucumber in that photo before the hour was up.

After sending her the touched up photo, I pressed a bit as to the "why" just for my own sanity.

I was informed that her "Instagram Husband" doesn't pay close attention to little details so some of her recent photos were less than flattering.

Like any normal person I asked what the fuck an "Instagram Husband" was.

For those also wondering, it's a husband who takes "cute" pictures of his wife for her Instagram feed.

I know, I regretted asking almost as soon as I asked but now we know.

After that exchange, I needed something to rinse my brain and get some other thoughts moving up there so I put myself back to work.

I took some of those newly milled posts we made, dug some holes, and set the outside wall for our new greenhouse.

With concrete drying in the holes, Teresa took the yard sweep over the area where we did all the sawing to clean up the sawdust.

She ended our outside work by being goosed by a turkey. I believe that turkey moved to the front of the butcher list.

Later Teresa made supper as I made dessert...

Chocolate cake with chocolate frosting. It's a tad over done and I think a touch of chocolate ice cream might make a great topper.

Until next time,
Most of us will live long enough to have no idea what the next generation is talking about... Think twice before you ask them to explain.

YEAR OF THE PLAGUE DAY 243:

Three inches to the north and three inches to the east, that's how far the old red barn leans. It makes building onto or making repairs to it interesting.

Last winter, the barn was unusable until spring because we could not get the doors open. The door is on the north side and the door opens out which means we stay drifted shut most of the winter.

Until yesterday that is. Yesterday Teresa and I removed the old falling down barn door, built a frame that was level, and built a whole new set of doors that open in.

We even managed to get a coat of paint on the doors before Teresa and I ventured out on a date night for the first time since March of this year.

An old highschool friend (sorry Casey, it's true, we're old) was playing live music just a few miles down the road so we got on our Sunday best and headed over for supper and some live music.

We had a good time, met some new people, and reminisced with some old friends. If that ain't a good date night, I ain't sure what is.

At about 11PM (that's like 4AM in old people time) we headed home for some rest so we could get back to working on the barn in the morning.

By "we" I mean "me". Teresa helped a heap, but not until almost 11 when she made it out of bed. Those late nights are tough on us!

Today it was time to get back after the greenhouse build on the south side of the barn.

I made some rough adjustments to our posts with the chainsaw, framed in the walls and made the rough openings for all the windows.

I had the first wall up before Teresa made it out to help and by then, the turkeys were glued to the fence watching the build like an episode of deadliest catch.

With Teresa's help, we were able to get the header plate up, the remaining wall sections, and the first two rafters hung before we called it quits.

Oh, before we did call it quits, the goats needed a new feed bunk so we scrounged up a piece of old 12" PVC pipe and made 'em one.

I'm not sure they understand it's for eating out of and not sleeping in but I guess if they enjoy it, our job is done.

Until next time.
Winter is coming, it's time to start preparing.

YEAR OF THE PLAGUE DAY 251:

The past eight days have been quiet on social media but super busy in real life.

We started our little greenhouse build last week and we realized this week how much we underestimated the project and overestimated our skill level.

We were already off to a great start on framing it in. The next day I uncovered a stack of steel in the trees and used the chainsaw to clear enough brush to get it out and use it to start siding the greenhouse.

It took a considerable amount of effort, a full tank of gas in the saw, a large fire, and one broken finger nail but the steel pile was recovered and we were able to get some good pieces up on the greenhouse.

With the addition of some old windows we found in the barn, we were almost done and I'd be lying if I said I wasn't a little proud of the results so far.

My pride was quickly balanced out with humility...

As we cleaned up tools for the day, I realized the windows alone are not letting in enough sun to be an effective greenhouse in South Dakota.

A good chunk of that steel would have to come down and we'd have to get something see through to replace it.

Teresa and I both had a drink that night.

The next day we picked up some greenhouse siding, added a bit more framing for support, and started siding the greenhouse... Again.

We have a few finishing touches left and it's a completed project, one we are happy to see the end of.

Even the turkeys fell asleep watching us do stuff for the second time.

The goats have handled all the commotion pretty well. Hannah even named the other one. Keeping with the "name them after food" rule, she named them Cinnamon and Oreo.

Hannah also got to have her very first marching band event with her new school.

A lot of her larger marching band events have been canceled but she kicked off the year on Friday.

They even let the high school football team play before and after the marching band performance.

Considering the challenges the kids have faced already this year, they did really well and we had a lot of fun watching them.

Hannah is the section leader for the color guard and new school or not, she still speaks band geek so she fits right in and still loves it.

Saturday Teresa and I felt the first tingle of the holiday spirit so we ventured into town and bought up some decorations for the house.

We planned to buy a whole LOT more decorations until we saw the price of holiday decorations.

It was quickly apparent that we had not purchased holiday decor for our home since the late 90s. This stuff is priced like gold. We did still purchase a few choice pieces for inspiration.

It was expensive enough that we protected our investment by buckling it into the back seat with seatbelts before driving home.

Later that evening while we were busy outside, Liberty the golden retriever ate a patch of carpet in the living room.

I shit you not, I had to count to ten before I could make another decision or take action after walking in and seeing it.

An hour later, Liberty was calmly watching me cut out and replace that corner of carpet.

Until she makes it past the one year mark, I'm going to tell myself it's just her being a puppy and she'll out grow it.

Still stewing over the price of holiday decor, we once again took action...

With the confidence of someone who just finished building a

greenhouse using telephone poles, a pile of old steel from the trees, and a stack of trailer house windows, we decided we could build our own stinking holiday decor.

To the woodshop we went, and with materials we had laying around the property, we started making all sorts of fall decorations.

Liberty joined us in the shop (since she can't be trusted alone indoors), and tried to do her part by eating the extra corn stalks we were intending to use for our decorations.

It was a small price to pay to keep her occupied so we'll call it a win and move forward.

Thanks to Pinterest, we have at least half a dozen more fall decoration projects we can do with stuff we have laying around so there will be more fun stuff to come.

Until next time,
Enjoy the fall weather and take solace in the fact that 2020 is another day closer to over!

YEAR OF THE PLAGUE DAY 253:

The morning was almost cold enough to produce a frost. The coldest morning this fall by at least 20 degrees and it had all the inhabitants on edge.

Bubba the rooster for example was resting near the top of the coop as I entered the barn to do chores today. He was more vocal than usual and I could see he wasn't gonna shut up until I let him out.

I finished up with the turkeys as quickly as I could and returned to let Bubba and the Bellas out for the day.

The hens all waddled out the door and free from the barn and Bubba stalked past me like an upset inmate who missed his yard time yesterday.

Within moments he was latched onto the wing of one of the hens and terrorized her for half a minute as she ran a circle squawking and trying to free her wing from his beak.

I stayed out of it. I minded my own business and continued on with chores. I figure they have a pecking order and I want no part of interfering so I look forward to my remaining tasks and ignore the squawking hens as they deal with the bully rooster.

As I finish up my tasks and return to the front of the barn, I'm greeted by the hens as usual and they seem to be much more calm and collected than when I left them.

I give them their usual good morning greetings and turn to head back to the house and the rest of my day.

A sharp pinch on my left calf muscle jolts me from my internal thoughts and I complete a jump that both propels me vertical and in a circle towards the source of my pain.

Bubba...

The rooster had sprinted towards me when I turned my back and had pecked me right on the leg. Seeing me launch up and around did little to temper his attack.

He saw the surprise in my eyes and mistook it for fear so he launched another offensive at my other leg this time.

My already stinging left leg was faster than his beak and my boot missed his feathered ass by a mear inch. It was enough though.

He turned tail and headed back to the safety of the hens and I headed back to the safety of the house while looking over my shoulder all the way there.

I ain't one to hold a grudge but I've put Teresa on notice, one more attack and I will be adjusting our weekly menu to include rooster.

Until next time,
Be careful who you trust in this Post-Rona world.

YEAR OF THE PLAGUE DAY 254:

Let's take a moment today and celebrate those who work from home and are still employed during this pandemic.

It's easy to brush these home workers off as the lucky few. After all, they still have jobs and they can work in their boxers all day.

But there's a darker side to this work from home racket that is never spoken of. Let me take you on a journey of my work from home experience today...

Shortly after lunch I had a Skype meeting scheduled with a business associate. I was half done with my day by this time and I was ready to have this call finished so I could jump into the remaining work on my plate.

The call started well, the meeting was productive and we were nearing the end of the call. We just were not nearing the end fast enough.

My stomach started to give me the traditional warning signs that a visit to the crapper was eminent. A bead of sweat formed on my brow and I started working the problem from both ends.

I tried to hurry the call along with little success and at the same time I tried to clench up and push the inevitable off as long as possible.

I stayed composed... calm... professional even considering the situation at hand. Ultimately, the outcome was not in my control and I had no choice but to head for the restroom while still on my call.

I put my phone on speaker and muted the microphone while my business associate talked at length about a project we were working on.

I was never so happy to hear someone talk for that long.

I completed my business as quietly as I could, which was not overly quiet, I may owe that toilet an apology. Then I flushed, cleaned up, and exited the restroom.

On my way back to my office I glanced at my phone to take it off mute and realized I had missed the mute button the first time.

I was loud and clear through the whole dump run and flush.

My business associate was gracious and said nothing, but he ended the call shortly after I flushed and it felt a bit rushed.

At the time, I figured maybe he had to get to the restroom but now I know, he was simply embarrassed for me.

Sooooooo, next time you think work from home people have it easy, ask yourself when was the last time you had a team meeting while taking a crap!

Until next time,
ALWAYS double check when you mute a phone!!!

YEAR OF THE PLAGUE DAY 257:

In an attempt to revisit my midwestern roots, Teresa and I traveled to Nebraska this weekend to spend a day with mom and dad.

The experience explained a lot about how I became the man I am today. It also made me wonder how I lived long enough to become a man at all.

That said, if you're ever in Nebraska, I'd highly recommend adding Deb and Al's house to your vacation stop overs. There is not a single attraction in the tristate area with as much excitement.

For example...

Dad decided we should jump on the golf cart and go check some game trail cameras. It sounded like an innocent, uneventful activity for an afternoon so I accepted the invite and we headed out the back door.

A few minutes later we had an old eclectic golf cart pulled out of the shed and I was comfortably sitting in the seat beside him.

With a moccasin covered foot, Al pressed the go pedal and we shot up a pretty steep hill to exit his yard onto an old country road.

Immediately Al jerked the wheel to the left and turned the cart around to face the steep hill again. "Your mother didn't charge the cart" he informed me, "so we don't have enough battery to make the trip".

Then Al pressed the go pedal once again to bring us back down that steep hill. Just as we start our descent, I see the other moccasined foot holding what should have been the brake pedal to the floor but we were NOT slowing down.

I think Al recognized my distress and he quickly set my mind at ease with an explanation.

"Brakes don't work" he informed me in a tone that showed he not only knew that before heading down the hill but that he was not worried about it either.

"Don't worry" he told me then. "I know how long it takes to stop on its own". Meaning, he's done this before and even without brakes, He knows the distance it takes to stop a moving golf cart rolling down a steep hill.

Now I ain't no physics professor but adding an extra two hundred pounds of scared redneck to the cart might extend that distance by a smidge.

He called it though, true to his word the cart stopped well short of the shed I was sure we would slam into.

He let me exit the seat, put the cart away, and plugged it in "the way your mother should have" he informed me.

The game trail cameras would have to wait. We had no other choice but to head back into the house and let mom know she let us all down by not charging the cart.

Deb listened calmly to the accusation before launching a counter attack and letting Al know he could go walk a dog.

"That's your cart, yours and the dogs" he informed her.

"Then don't worry about it being charged" she replied with a look that dared him to keep pursuing this line of conversation.

With a look of exasperation he turned to me and told me, "You can't tell her anything, she knows everything that can be known!".

To which Deb replied with barely a breath of pause between, "The shut up and listen damn it!".

Holding in a laugh I exchanged looks with Teresa and I could see she was having just as much fun at this attraction as I was. If we could give mom and dad's house a five star on Yelp, we'd have done it!

I won't give away all the exciting things you can see here but comical exchanges, arguments with Alexa, and bouts of calling inanimate objects all sorts of obscenities are just a few things that will keep you entertained.

All in all, it's a must see and I highly recommend it!

Until next time,
Check on your parents from time to time, sanity slips quickly in quarantine.

YEAR OF THE PLAGUE DAY 260:

There has been a lot accomplished around the Eckert household over the past few days. I moved all the telephone poles to their winter home, mowed the yard for the final time this year, and broke the new mower badly enough that it will now be one of my winter projects.

That was all pretty exciting, but our crowning accomplishment was getting our new furniture. Our new home has a much larger living room than our old home so we upgraded from seating for five to seating for ten.

During our shopping experience we talked ourselves into the electric recliners. We've had the manual kind forever and the older we get the harder those manual foot stools are to kick back into place.

We had no idea until last night that our thinking was flawed and we were overlooking some of the drawbacks to this new technology.

For example, you can strike a pretty imposing pose and scare the bejezus out of a misbehaving dog or child by slamming your footstool down as you launch yourself out of the seat ready for battle.

Try that shit in an electric recliner.

Your temper spikes, you make the decision to go on the offencive, you give the standard verbal lashing to your prey, and then you start fumbling for the right buttons.

First your headrest pushes forward making you bow your neck forward in an almost submissive bow, then you're heading backwards to fully lounged position.

Now you're really pissed...

You finally locate the correct buttons and press them with all your might as if the pressure from your ghost white finger tip can be felt by your prey.

Slowly your footstool descends as the misbehaving dog calmly walks away towards the dog door as if there's no worries in the world.
At this point the dog believes I had a stroke and dismissed me as harmless.

I'll be stocking the end tables with projectiles to reestablish dominance in the home this week.

The good news is we are ready to host Thanksgiving and we have lots of new (slow) seating!

Until next time,
Technology comes with a cost, buyer beware.

YEAR OF THE PLAGUE DAY 265:

Apparently humans are not the only thing rioting (aka: peaceful protesting). Mother nature is following suit and having riots of her own this year.

We had a welcome insect swarm cross our yard for about two days this week. Monarch butterflies were so thick on the trees it looked like the leaves had changed colors already.

It was a pretty cool sight to see and I was able to sit and enjoy it for a short time before life called me back to action.

With the official first day of fall upon us, we finally struck a deal on a new snowblower for the tractor. Winter should be much easier to handle this year once I do some maintenance on it..

We even made a bundle deal and got a tiller for next spring in anticipation of our very first real garden in our new home. The tiller needs some TLC but seems to be functional.

The gentleman we purchased the equipment from delivered them on a flatbed trailer and it was up to me to get them off the trailer and on the ground.

I have no idea how much this stuff weighs but an 8ft snowblower is a mammoth piece of equipment for someone like me and I was sufficiently intimidated by the job.

Figuring the old man got the blower and tiller ON the trailer, I started asking questions as to the best way to remove them with my loader.

In no time at all he had me positioned with the tractor and was tossing chains around stuff. Seconds later he was giving hand signals that I assume he thought I should know and we were moving steel.

I interpreted the hand signals the best I could while watching where he and Teresa were so if I did misinterpret, no one had to die.

Smooth as butter we had the new toys unloaded and I was able to pick his brain for many other neat tricks only an old farmer would know.

I may pretend to look at more equipment at his place later this week just to solicit free advice.

After unloading and getting the old fella on his way, I was pretty eager to dig into the new attachments but other things on the todo list were demanding my attention.

The new chickens we got at auction (along with two ducks) for example... Today was their first day outside in the chicken run.

They shared the run with the turkeys and goats and they were all getting along about as well as you'd imagine for the first day.

Then I had the bright idea of tossing some over ripe tomatoes in with them as a treat.

As soon as the first tomato hit the ground, the chicken run boiled like a small pond full of piranha. Tiny little chickens were standing off the goats, turkeys were pulling chicken feathers, and ducks were running in circles keeping the frenzy going.

Within seconds there was no trace of tomato left and the carnage calmed a bit. The only thing I can compare the whole scene to is a freshly stocked Target store in downtown Minneapolis. Insanity comes to mind.

As if that's not enough excitement for the day, Teresa and I settled into the house this afternoon and realized we were in the middle of yet another swarm of what looked like ladybugs. We found out they are called Asian Beetles and they tend to swarm in the fall.

They are so thick outside it looks like a city sized bee hive got kicked over. We even had several get into the house when we tried to enter or exit the front door.

Teresa wasn't about to put up with that and decided to stand on the front porch with a can of flying insect repellent and take as many down as she could.

It was a lot like watching someone fly a kite in a tornado. She was no match for the biblical sized plague but she was gonna do her damndest to hold her front porch.

Until next time,
May your days be safe and swarm free

YEAR OF THE PLAGUE DAY 269:

We had a few errands to run in town tonight so Teresa opted out of cooking and we decided to try out one of the few places in town we have not eaten at yet.

By all accounts it was a nice enough place, fairly clean inside and out and the food smelled appetizing.

We approached the door and I held it open for Teresa like a gentleman and we entered the well lit eatery.

It was busy, a little noisey, and the only seating available was at the bar not 30 feet from a young couple with a crying baby.

The young mom worked to quiet the child as dad looked around the room to see if they were bothering anyone. They certainly were not, everyone was concentrating on their meals.

We slid into the only two bar stools left at the bar and waited about 10 minutes for the owner of the establishment to get us menus and take our drink order.

He seemed like a nice enough fella and the wait was forgivable considering how busy they were. We gave him our drink orders and briefly discussed the options on the menu.

Both Teresa and I settled on wings. Teresa was going to try two different kinds and get a side of pickle fries and I was going to get traditional buffalo wings with fries. Or so I thought.

The option for normal wings was NOT on the menu. I asked the owner what he had that was the closest to a "Mild" buffalo wing and he promptly steered me towards a selection simply named "HOT".

"Yea"? I asked, to which he quickly replied "yep", and I put my trust in the man as I confirmed my order.

Looking over the menu while our order was being made I could clearly see the levels of hotness climbed vertically up the menu with "Hot" being the hottest.

Still, I asked the man and if anyone would know it must be him I told myself.

15 minutes later our order was brought out and placed in front of us. The smell of my wings alone prompted the first few beads of sweat to form on my brow.

I arranged my food, wings directly in front of me, fries to my right, said a quick and silent prayer and took my first bite.

Now if you're not a spicy food eater, let me share something with you... There's two kinds of hot. The hot that kind of sneaks up on you and the hot that hits right dagom now like a hot poker in the eye.

These wings were the later.

Within seconds I could feel the sweat making its way down my face and I'm sure I turned three shades whiter.

Teresa saw my distress and I swear I heard a giggle as she side eyed me like I was a disney villain finally getting his due.

Then and there I made the decision to finish what I started. I ordered these "mild" wings according to the owner and I was dang sure gonna finish them.

Dipping wing number two into some ranch dressing I reluctantly moved the fork towards my burning tongue. I snatched the mild wing from the fork and chewed then swallowed as quickly as I could without choking.

Then I realized my lip was burning. I dripped a bit of the sauce on my lip and the spice was actually making my lip feel like it was on fire!

At this point the couple with the baby were more concerned that I was disturbing people with my crying than their baby.

I won't bore you with the details of the remaining four wings. Let's just say that by the time I had finished them, I couldn't eat my fries because just the feel of something touching my tongue made my whole face hurt.

All the while Teresa was laughing. Actually laughing out loud at me.

At one point the owner stopped to ask how everything was to which I replied "Fucking HOT" with a sweat soaked fase and accusing eyes.

He simply shook his head yes as if to affirm what I now knew and walked away with a smile I now knew belonged to a sadist.

I emptied my second soft drink, paid the bill, and we left from the same side door we entered. This time I did NOT feel obligated to hold the door for Teresa. If she could laugh and walk, she could hold her own damn door.

I already had a new set of problems to worry about. I needed to use the restroom but I was afraid to use the restroom until I washed my hands several times to avoid any accidental "mild" wing sauce getting where it didn't belong.

We hightailed it home, Hands were washed, tears were dried, and we swore for the sake of our marriage we would not speak of these events again.

Until next time,
It's worth occasionally asking, how well do you really know your spouse?

YEAR OF THE PLAGUE DAY 273:

How I planned today... Wake up, butcher turkeys, got to bed.

How my day actually happened...

My phone rang at 6:45 AM this morning waking me from whatever random dream my brain had on repeat for the night.

I was not ready to be awake just yet and the interruption was proven even more aggravating when I looked at the phone and realized it was a junk call.

I should have realized there and then that my day was gonna be one of "those" days.

Twenty two minutes later, Hannah left for school and came back into the house shortly after leaving it. Her car would not start which loosely translates to "dad, you have a problem to solve".

Teresa and Hannah beat me back out to the garage and had the battery charger all hooked up before I could even get my pants and boots on.

Unfortunately, the battery was just fine but the new starter we just put in was stuck and not engaging with the flywheel to start the car.

For as long as there have been starters, there have been stuck starters so there were a few tried and true tricks I could try.

Trick one... smack the crap out of the starter with a hammer and see if that works. We repeated this trick a few times and still no luck.

Trick two... curse at the car. A lot. Nope, that one didn't work either but I repeated it a few more times just in case.

Trick three... turn the key on, turn the wheels side to side, cycle through the gears, and roll the car a few inches back and forth while in neutral. BAM! That one did the trick.

The girls looked at me like I just called lightning from a sunny sky and I pretended I had planned it that way the whole time.

The way this day was going, I was gonna take my wins where I could get them, even if they were made up.

By 10AM we had a guy here trenching in copper line and dropping off a new propane tank for our wood shop. No more running back and forth to fill 100lb bottles this winter!!

We didn't have this planned for today but we were not going to waste the chance to get it done.

While he was here, I had him dig a trench from the wood shop to the barn so we could add power to the barn for the animals this winter.

As he set to digging, I started getting things set up for Teresa and I to butcher our turkeys. This included building a new killing cone because the cone for chickens is way too small.

Once I was set up for the birds, I ran the conduit for the power wire that would feed the barn. With some help from Teresa, we got the wire ran and buried so that was another project off our list.

Then it was time for the 2020 turkey harvest.

It has only been a few months since we butchered chickens so we felt pretty confident this was gonna go well.

Honestly, turkeys are just larger versions of chickens right? How hard can it be?

Turkey #1: I snatched him from the pen, placed him upside down in the new killing cone I made, removed his head and we were off to a good start.

After he settled and our water was up to temp, I dipped him to loosen the feathers and headed over to the plucker. I was worried the bird was too big for the plucker but it worked pretty well.

Ten minutes later, with Teresa's help, the first turkey was cleaned up and cooling off in the ice cold cooler.

Sure the turkeys were heavier and a bit more bulky to work with but things were going pretty well at this point.

Turkey #2: Much the same as turkey one. This turkey went pretty smooth and our confidence was kinda up there.

Turkey #3: Slid into the killing cone easy as can be and I removed the head so it could bleed out before going to the scalding pot.

Then life decided I needed to be humbled again so my day took a turn. It turns out that if you place a turkey in the cone with its back towards the post, things go pretty well.

If on the other hand you place the bird in with its back towards you, it can use the post as leverage when it starts kicking and shit gets real, real quick.

I'm sure most of you are familiar with the dance a chicken does when its head is removed. That in no way prepares you for what happens when you do the same with a turkey.

Within moments of removing the head I could see something was different with this bird. It was going to come right out the top of the cone and I knew I had to act fast.

As I lunged towards the bird, it pushed off with both feet and dislodged itself from the cone just as I reached it.

My hands wrapped around air where there was once a bird and my face was met with a series of rapid fire wing slaps from a wing the size of a dinner plate.

Then the claws struck as the bird descended, still not to the ground yed. One scratch on my left hand, one on my right arm, and one on my left knee before the bird touched down.

The moment the bird hit the ground, it exploded right back up into the air and the dance began again. All the while blood was pumping out like a yard sprinkler.

After about a minute of this, I finally had the bird pinned down and under control. The damage had already been done though.

I was feeling scratches and bruises all over, I was covered from the top of my head to the bottom of my boots in turkey blood and I could tell Teresa was doing her best not to laugh.

It didn't work, she laughed.

The important thing was that I learned something. The remaining birds were done with their back to the pole and we finished without any further problems.

We did eight turkeys in about three hours and they averaged about 16lbs per bird fully dressed.

If that wasn't reward enough, we saved the gizzards which were the size of Teresa's hand!

Until next time,
Learn from your mistakes, and don't turn your back on a woman who laughs at your misfortune!

YEAR OF THE PLAGUE DAY 277:

We had been anticipating the possibilities of this day for weeks, today was the exotic livestock auction in Mitchell South Dakota.

Lions, tigers, and bears had been dancing in my head since the day we heard about the event.

Add that to the fact that this was the perfect environment to spot that bitch Carol Baskin and you have yourself a hum-dinger of an event planned.

Unfortunately, Carol Baskin was busy on Dancing With The Stars and there was not a lion, tiger, or bear to be found.

We did however get to see some pretty cool stuff.

Kangaroos, wallabies, porcupines, armadillos, ostriches, emues, and all sorts of non-typical livestock were paraded by us for inspection.

A mini-jersey cow gave us its impression of a run away fire hose and a miniature hereford calf convinced our cousin Derek to take it home and in the process made a little girl cry because she really wanted it instead.

Several times I had to ask myself, "what the hell would you even do with that", to prevent an impulse bid on some cute but impractical critter for the homestead.

In the end, we had a pretty good day and I did make two purchases and neither of them requires food nor shits on my property...

A red cedar bench and a red cedar porch swing are the spoils of war for Teresa and I but the memories of the time we "almost" bought a mini goat will live on well past the outdoor furniture.

Until next time,
Expectations are always greater than reality and mini cows are exactly as cute as they sound.

YEAR OF THE PLAGUE DAY 286:

The turkeys are in the freezer, the goats are scheduled to hit the locker in January, and I showed restraint by not buying any animals at the exotic action a week ago.

All that felt like a great reason to reward myself by bringing a few new residents to the homestead this week.

One noisy rooster who we've renamed to Bumper and four hens who lay the coolest green and blue eggs for us.

After piecing a coop together with odds and ends laying around the place we got the new birds settled in and started collecting eggs on the very first day.

Our goal is to have 8 hens and 1 rooster for this particular coop so the first dozen or so eggs went straight to the incubator and are due to hatch on the 2nd of November. We'll see how many make it.

Meanwhile, Teresa and I made our first prototype kitchen chair and Teresa took it upon herself to knock out the remaining four chairs solo.

Yep, I know how lucky I am... She tells me all the time!

She's close to perfect but NOT QUITE there. I captured video proof of her playing with her food today.

Until next time,
Check in on your animal hoarding friends, this pandemic is tough on us!

YEAR OF THE PLAGUE DAY 295:

There's little doubt that 2020 is for the birds and this past week has convinced me that is exactly as it should be.

The week started with a quick shop project to make some bird carriers to haul our ducks and one chicken to auction. From the bike tire hinges to the old cabinet handle they were made completely from the scrap pile.

The birds all sold and after paying the auction house cut we made our first $6 on poultry farming and made a name for ourselves in the fowl farming community.

Now that I have the attention of the major players in the bird industry, I'm stepping up my game and hatching a few more birds for our flock.

We got 14 eggs in the store bought incubator and another 16 ready to go into my new homemade incubator. Fingers crossed we get our first batch of peeping fluff nuggets on the second of November.

We'll be practicing selective breeding for positive traits such as intelligence. One of our hens is clearly not qualified to participate in the program. I can't seem to keep her out of the live traps meant to protect her from critters.

I'm tempted to give her a name but with her disqualification I'm afraid she's destined for the crock pot.

On a brighter note, I've discovered the best thing about raising the turkeys this year was a big bag of homemade turkey jerky. This stuff is like crack and we are gonna need to hide the bag so we don't eat it all in a day.

Until next time,
When life gives ya chickens, keep your day job and trade them for turkey jerky!

YEAR OF THE PLAGUE DAY 301:

I went to bed last night feeling pretty lucky. In addition to all the cool looking birds we have around here, Teresa and I have been enjoying the company of a cardinal the past two days. She sits just outside our window.

I wasn't sure how that tingle of luck I felt was going to play out in the coming days but it didn't take long to find out.

Around 7:30 AM as I'm slipping into a pair of wool socks, listening to the coffee maker finish its given task, and getting ready to do my chores in the cold seven degree morning, my attention is pulled towards the back yard.

Liberty the cowardly golden retriever is barking like she lost her mind, and while it's not unusual for her to lose her mind, she doesn't usually bark quite like that. I knew something was up.

I stumbled to the back door and looked out to see what she was focused on and I don't see much of anything. Thinking she scared something off I quickly made my way to the front of the house and took a peek that way.

Then I see it, a doe (a deer, a female deer) standing in my tree row about 60 yards off my front porch. As luck would have it, I just got my first deer tag in over fifteen years and it was time to fill it.

I know, I said I had no room in the freezer, but this chubby fella has been eating and I figured by the time we got a deer, we'd have room.

Anyhow, with one boot on and one boot half on I grab my rifle and try to slide quietly onto the front porch, careful not to make a sound.

I'd have pulled it off too if it weren't for the dog barking behind me and the cat joejoe racing up the porch steps and greeting me with a million meow hello.

Like a trained sniper I keep my cool, take a knee and rest the rifle on the porch railing. Simultaneously I chamber a round, bring my prey into the scope, and click the safety off.

Then the goats see me. It's full on baaaahhh baaahhh baaaahhh until I go feed them now so I figure it's over for the hunt. I briefly consider swinging the scope to the goat pen but hold my position in the hopes of salvaging a shot.

My luck holds and the doe looks around but holds stead right where she is. I silently curse the dog, the cat, and the goats as I begin to squeeze the trigger.

In the next two breaths it was done. The blast from the rifle sent Liberty the golden retriever and joejoe the cat into panicked hiding and I watched as the doe took three steps and went down.

By the time I looked over the goats were back in the barn and my outlook on the day improved measurably. I give one quick caveman grunt to signify my dominance over my homestead and turn to go inside.

Before I could stand up and take the four steps back into the front door, Teresa was stumbling out of the bedroom half dressed wondering what kind of an idiot is shooting a cannon at 7:30 in the morning.

I stepped back inside, did a bit of explaining, regained my composure and my coffee, then finished getting dressed so I could finish chores which now included dressing out a deer.

By 2 PM the deer was in the freezer but not before a small bit was fried up for the taste test. By South Dakota white tail standards, this deer was embarrassingly small, but she tastes pretty dang good to us.

After remaining skittish for most of the day, Liberty finally calmed down and is back on watch duty. She may need treatment for PTSD but for now she's been cleared for duty.

Until next time,
If you can deer hunt from your porch, it sure saves a lot of hassle.

YEAR OF THE PLAGUE DAY 310:

The eggs we set in our incubator three weeks ago have finally hatched! This is our very first hatch from our own birds and Teresa and I were both pretty excited.

Over the past three weeks, I have worn a path in the ground marching from the house to the wood shop to check on the eggs.

I played it cool though, my excitement was pretty well masked and Teresa was a rock. I'm not sure she even visited the eggs until the end and showed little interest.

That is until week three...

On day 21 we put the eggs on lock down and shortly after we had our first chick trying to break free.

For the next four days Teresa and I were helicopter parents. In and out we went on an almost hourly basis from the time we woke up until we went to bed.

Each day a few more chicks hatched and each day we got to greet them and pull a few from the incubator into the brooder.

Teresa even face-timed (is that a word?) our oldest daughter and made her watch for thirty minutes as one of the last chicks hatched.

I think it's safe to say we are both crazy chicken folks and you have to admit, it's kinda cool to have a pet that craps breakfast and that you can eat if they don't behave.

Anywho, the first batch of chicks (minus a few we kept) are finding new homes on local farms and we can now officially add chicken farmer to our list of titles!

Until next time,
Whoever said "don't count your chickens before they hatch" never had to plan out brooder and coop space!

YEAR OF THE PLAGUE DAY 314:

This weekend Teresa and I salvaged a trailer load of lumber from a decommissioned porch. With lumber at an all time high this year we were determined to take advantage of a good deal even if it took some extra work.

After what felt like a full day of planing down, stripping edges, and cleaning up 2x6s we had enough to take on our first project with the reclaimed wood... our pantry!

Teresa emptied the small room off our kitchen, stripped the carpet from the floor, and had it painted yellow so quick that Georgia election officials have begun to study her in hopes of improving their 2024 performance.

Sunday we worked together to make thirty new shelf brackets to hold the new shelving in our pantry. That project started out a little rough as Teresa misfired the brad nailer and missed my left nipple by less than an inch.

While I've always considered myself a forward thinker, pierced nipples are still a bit too progressive for this guy so I took control of the nailer for the remainder of the project.

That bit finished, I took on my next project… A new brooder setup for our little chicken hatchery. We now have room for 60-80 chicks comfortably and we'll be selling day old chicks as well as 6 week old chicks in the coming months.

To that end, Teresa and I bounced names back and forth for hours in regards to our new chicken enterprise. After much discussion we settled on Empty Nest Acres.

Since kicking our adult children out of the nest has given us the freedom to live on an acreage and play with chickens we thought the name was fitting. Sorry not sorry kids!!

Meanwhile, our chickens were taking advantage of the fact that we had crazy high winds that blew over Teresa's bird feeder yesterday. At least the mess got cleaned up I guess.

Until next time,
Never hand your wife a loaded brad nailer!

YEAR OF THE PLAGUE DAY 316:

Yesterday mother nature declared it winter time for the second time this year. Snow fell from 9AM until 7PM, ice formed on the roads making it slick, and it was a great day to just stay indoors.

But we didn't.

Each and every snow fall is a great reminder that we no longer live in the suburbs. No plow trucks were coming by to take away the snow. I now had a whole lot of driveway and parking area to keep clear all winter so out into the cold I went.

I felt pretty confident. I had a beast of a machine in my tractor and snow blower. No amount of snow was gonna keep us bottled up.

What I realized pretty quickly was that beast of a machine is a real SOB when you're blowing snow without a cab.

By the time I finished up and came inside, I looked like a snowman and I'm certain my face had absorbed at least a few truck loads of blowing snow.

I may need to start saving up for a winter tractor and leave this one in the shed as my summer tractor.

I wonder if that's a thing? Do farmers have summer and winter tractors? I feel like they should now.

Either way, the job got done and I felt colder, older, and wiser for having done it. It was now time to warm up.

As I'm settling into my favorite chair with a blanket, Hannah our youngest starts making a fuss from the kitchen. Curious about her issue I asked what the problem was.

"The Keurig is out of water every time I try to use it" she informed me with an accusing glare. Apparently she was trying to make hot chocolate and filling the water on the Keurig was a bit more work than she signed up for.

"I know, it is for me too" I told her before shifting my attention back to more important matters, whatever was on TV at the moment.

As I got myself moving the next morning and prepared to make myself coffee, I chuckled to myself a little as I remembered the conversation with Hannah.

My chuckle was short lived though. Hannah had put just enough water in the Keurig to get her cup of hot chocolate out of it leaving me to deal with the empty container in the morning.

Lucky for her, she had already escaped the house and left for school by this time. I may however wait until she returns and pile a load of snow behind her car with the loader.

Until next time,

CORY ECKERT

Never underestimate a teenage girl.

YEAR OF THE PLAGUE DAY 328:

Teresa and I are on our game today, chores are done early, birds are fat and happy, we have a customer coming to pick up some baby chicks, and the calm morning prompted Teresa to get the garbage burning.

In a back-to-the-basics kind of year like 2020 you really can't ask for much more can ya?

As we were settling back into the house to warm up, we even noticed the cats were all on the porch by the front door. How cute is that!

One of them is even raising a stink in what seems like an attempt to get us to let her in. "Meeee Yooooow, Meeee Yooooow" over and over.

About then, our customer shows up for her birds and Teresa, myself, and our customer all realize at about the same time that "Meeee Yoooow" was the cat's version of a fire alarm!

The cat's house and some dead trees were on FIRE!

Teresa's garbage burning turned into a cat-tastrophy and was burning down the cat's winter shelter and spreading into the trees.

A year ago I'm not sure we would have handled the situation as well. Being a tried and true farmer over the past year however has instilled in us a "get-shit-done" kind of attitude and we quickly adapted to our new roles as firefighters.

I tossed Teresa a fire extinguisher from the woodshop while I grabbed another from the metal shop. Teresa started blasting the flames with her fire extinguisher as I was quickly let down by mine not working.
I wouldn't be defeated though, I turned and quickstepped to the barn for hoses. Little by little I had hoses strung and Teresa was connecting them to water and the situation was beginning to come under control.

I continued to hose down the fire and asked Teresa to escort our horrified customer to the barn to retrieve her new chicks.

After our customer left, I had to do some ax work on the logs and cat house to get some hot spots from the centers but I think we did well in our firefighter training and we are thankful nothing further burned.

Until next time,
When you hear "Meeee Yooooow, Meeee Yooooow, Meeee Yooooow", stop what you're doing and look for flames!

YEAR OF THE PLAGUE DAY 333:

Twas the day before, the day before, the month of Christmas and all around the farm,
The farmers were busy creating old Christmas charm.

Thanksgiving is over and Christmas is near,
The year is almost over and it can kiss our rear.

Some lights were strung here and ribbons tied there,
Decorations were hung with barely a care.

There were a few squabbles but they weren't all that bad,
This farmer couple seldom gets mad.

They make a great team and can weather the storm,
Even this year when upside down is the norm.

Anyway, I should really get goin,
There's work to do here before it starts snowin.

We'll see ya, goodbye, we out,
Now where did I put those pills for my gout…..

CORY ECKERT

Until next time,
May your holiday season suck less than the rest of 2020.

YEAR OF THE PLAGUE DAY 346:

After several days of procrastination, today was finally the day. It had to be done and there was no putting it off any longer...

Bumper the rooster had a date with the stew pot.

My internal demons were at war with each other. On one hand, the older I get the harder it is to take a life. On the other hand, I'm fat and I get hungry easy so there's that.

But what do you do with a stringy old rooster? I dare say we've found the perfect answer to that age old question...

Step 1. Gut, skin, and debone
Step 2. Grind all salvageable meat
Step 3. Use meat to make super delicious jerky!
Step 4. Use carcass to make super delicious chicken stock!

If all that wasn't a big enough gift from Bumper the rooster, his departure had us rearranging cages today and we found a stash of eggs!

I'd have to say Bumpers funeral food is top notch.

On a brighter note, the dirt work has begun for our new chicken coop and it should be operational by Christmas. Obviously that won't do bumper much good but I'm sure the hens will be excited.

Also, Hannah (the sometimes cranky teenager who lives with us) is becoming a pretty good photographer and she has been contracted to do all our bird photoshoots.

Until next time,
Sometimes choking your chicken can lead to good things!

YEAR OF THE PLAGUE DAY 350:

Today was C.O.L.D... The kind of cold that brings your fathers analogies back into use. Sayings we all know and love like...

It's colder than a witch's tit in a brass bra.
It's colder than a well diggers ass.
It's colder than a penguin's pecker.
Or It's so cold Bill Clinton is sleeping with his own wife.

Thanks dad for bringing culture and variety to a young mind.

Now, even though it was cold enough to freeze the balls off a pool table, we had stuff that needed doing so we bundled up and pushed through.

Our biggest accomplishment was getting our new shed (soon to be chicken coop) in place and giving it some Christmas spirit.

By the time we finished, Teresa could cut glass with her nipples and shrinkage had given me a man-gina so we made for the house to warm up.

A warm bowl of chili, fresh corn bread muffins, and hot chocolate are in the works as a reward for a job well done.

Until next time,
Stay warm out there and keep it classy folks!

YEAR OF THE PLAGUE DAY 360:

The year is officially coming to an end and I'm as certain as this winter is long that our adventures are only just beginning.

If you made it through the whole year with us and didn't get too triggered or offended by the contents of our daily life, THANK YOU for being you and for spending time with the likes of us!

Teresa and I feel extremely blessed to be living the life we built together and it's made so much better by the people who are part of it.

Until next time,
…

AFTERWORD

Thank you for taking the time to read about our adventures.

For images and videos to help bring the daily stories to life, be sure to check out our Facebook group.

Images available at - https://www.facebook.com/groups/pandemicinthemidwest

We also continue to post more daily ramblings so join today and don't miss out!

ABOUT THE AUTHOR

Cory Eckert

I, Cory Eckert, am the author of very little, absolutely nothing of note in fact.

This collection of ramblings was done out of boredom and never intended for public release until I was pressured into it by my peers.

Please buy my book, I owe people money.

Made in United States
Troutdale, OR
08/18/2024

22076396R00127